Regent's Park

About the Author

Paul Rabbitts has over twenty-three years of
experience in designing, managing and restoring
urban parks across the UK, from the Scottish Borders
to the South East of England. A qualified Landscape
Architect and current Head of Parks for a South East
Local Authority, he is also a published author and
regular contributor to journals and periodicals. His
other books include *Bandstands* in the popular Shire
series. Paul lives in Leighton Buzzard.

Vanish

SOPHIE JORDAN

Vanish

A Firelight Novel

OXFORD

UNIVERSITY PRESS

OXFORD
UNIVERSITY PRESS

Great Clarendon Street, Oxford OX2 6DP

Oxford University Press is a department of the University of Oxford.
It furthers the University's objective of excellence in research, scholarship,
and education by publishing worldwide in

Oxford   New York

Auckland   Cape Town   Dar es Salaam   Hong Kong   Karachi
Kuala Lumpur   Madrid   Melbourne   Mexico City   Nairobi
New Delhi   Shanghai   Taipei   Toronto

With offices in

Argentina   Austria   Brazil   Chile   Czech Republic   France   Greece
Guatemala   Hungary   Italy   Japan   Poland   Portugal   Singapore
South Korea   Switzerland   Thailand   Turkey   Ukraine   Vietnam

Oxford is a registered trade mark of Oxford University Press
in the UK and in certain other countries

British Library Cataloguing in Publication Data

Data available

ISBN: 978-0-19-275654-1

1 3 5 7 9 10 8 6 4 2

Printed in Great Britain

Paper used in the production of this book is a natural,
recyclable product made from wood grown in sustainable forests.
The manufacturing process conforms to the environmental
regulations of the country of origin.

For my agent, Maura—for being more than an agent

The heart that truly loves never forgets.

—*Proverbs*

Sometimes I dream of falling.

Of course, I start out flying in these dreams. Because that's what I do. What I am. What I love.

A few weeks ago, I would have said it's what I love most in the world, but a lot has changed since then. Everything, really.

In these dreams, I'm racing through the sky, free as I'm supposed to be. And then something happens because suddenly I'm descending in a tailspin. I clutch air, my screams eaten up by angry wind. I plummet. A human without wings. Just a girl, not a draki at all. Powerless. Lost.

I feel that way now: I'm falling, and I can do nothing. I can stop none of it. I'm caught up in the old nightmare.

I always wake before I hit ground. That's been my salvation. Only tonight I'm not dreaming. Tonight I hit the ground. And it's every bit as painful as I expected.

I rest my cheek against the cool glass of the window and watch the night rush past me. As Cassian drives, my eyes strain through the motionless dark, skimming over rock yards and stucco houses, searching for an answer, a reason for everything that's happened.

The world seems to hold its breath as we slow for a stop sign. My gaze drifts to the dark sky above us. A deep, starless sea beckoning, promising sanctuary.

Mom's voice drifts forward from the backseat, low and crooning as she talks to Tamra, trying to coax a response from her. I peel my cheek from the glass and glance over my shoulder. Tamra shivers in Mom's arms. Her eyes stare vacantly ahead; her skin corpse pale.

'Is she OK?' I ask again, because I have to say something. I have to know. Did I do this to her? Is this, too, my fault? 'What's wrong with her?'

Mom frowns and shakes her head at me like I shouldn't speak. I've let them both down. I broke the unbreakable rule. I revealed my true form to humans—worse, hunters—and we will all pay for the mistake. The knowledge presses on me, a crushing weight that sinks me deep into my seat. I face forward again, trembling uncontrollably. I cross my arms, pinning my hands at my sides as though that might still them.

Cassian warned me there would be a reckoning for this night's work, and I wonder whether it's already begun. I've lost Will. Tamra is sick or in shock or maybe something worse. Mom can hardly look at me. My every breath is misery, the events of the night burning inside my eyelids. Me, shedding my human skin and manifesting in front of Will's family. My desperate flight through crackling dry air to reach him. But if I hadn't manifested—hadn't flown to Will's side—he'd be dead, and I couldn't bear that thought. I'll never see

Will again, no matter his promise to find me, but at least he's alive.

Cassian says nothing beside me. He did all the talking he needed to do to get Mom in the car with us, to make her understand returning with him to the home we fled is the only viable option. His fingers hold tight to the steering wheel, his knuckles white. I doubt he'll relax his grip until we're free and clear of Chaparral. Probably not until we're safely back in the pride. *Safe.* I strangle on a laugh—or it could be a sob. Will I ever feel *safe* again?

The town flies past, houses thinning out as we near the edge of town. We'll be gone soon. Free of this desert and the hunters. Free of Will. This last thought claws fresh the already bleeding wound in my heart, but there's nothing to be done about it. Could there ever have been a future for us? A draki and a draki hunter? *A draki hunter with the blood of my kind running through his veins.*

That part of it all still stumbles through my head, refusing to penetrate. I can't close my eyes without seeing the flash of his shimmering purple blood in the night. Like my own. My head aches, struggling to accept this terrible truth. No matter how valid Will's explanation, no matter that I still love him, it doesn't change the fact that the stolen blood of my kind pumps through his veins.

Cassian exhales slowly as we leave the city limits.

'Well, that's that,' Mom murmurs as the distance grows between us and Chaparral.

I turn to find her looking back through the rear window. She's leaving all her hopes for a better future in Chaparral. It's where we were making a fresh start, away from the pride. And now we're headed back into their midst.

'I'm sorry, Mom,' I say, not just because I should, but because I mean it.

Mom shakes her head, opening her mouth to speak, but gets nothing out.

'We've got trouble,' Cassian announces. Straight ahead, several cars block the road, forcing us to slow.

'It's them,' I manage to utter past numb lips as Cassian pulls closer.

'Them?' Mom demands. 'Hunters?'

I give a hard nod. Hunters. *Will's family.*

Glaring headlights pierce the dark and illuminate Cassian's face. His gaze flicks to the rearview mirror and I can tell he's contemplating turning back around, running for it in the other direction. But it's too late for that—one car moves to block our escape and several figures step in front of our car. Cassian slams on the brakes, his hands flexing on the steering wheel, and I know he's fighting the impulse to mow them down. I strain for a glimpse of Will, sensing him, knowing he's there, among them somewhere.

Hard, biting voices shout at us to get out of the car. I hold still, my fingers a hot singe on my bare legs, pressing so deeply—as though I were trying to reach my draki buried underneath.

A fist bangs down on our hood, and then I see it—the outline of a gun in the gloom.

Cassian's gaze locks with mine, communicating what I already know. We have to survive. Even if it means doing only what our kind *can* do. That very thing I already did, that got us in this jam tonight in the first place. And why not? It's not like we can reveal our secret *more*.

Nodding, I move, climbing out of the car to face our enemies.

Will's cousin Xander steps ahead of the others thrusting his smug face toward me. 'Did you really think you could get away?'

Crushing pain fills my chest, anger at what these monsters have cost me tonight. Ash gathers at the back of my throat, and I let the acrid burn build, preparing myself for whatever may come.

A hunter beats a fist on the back window, shouting at Mom and Tamra. 'Get out of the car!'

Mom steps out with as much dignity as she can muster, pulling Tamra with her. My sister's grown even paler since Big Rock; her wheezy breath scrapes the air. Her amber brown eyes, the same as mine, look cloudy, almost filmy as she stares into space. Her lips part, but no words escape. I step close and lend a hand, helping Mom support her. Tam's icy to the touch, her skin not skin at all. Chilled marble.

Cassian faces Xander, regal as the prince he essentially is. Light glints off the purple and black strands of his hair.

I moisten my lips, wondering how I can convince Xander he didn't see me manifest. 'What do you want?'

Will's cousin stabs a finger at me. 'We'll start with you—whatever the hell you are.'

'Get away from her,' Cassian commands.

Xander's attention swings to Cassian. 'And then we'll move to you, big guy . . . and how it is you fell off that cliff with Will and don't have a scratch.'

'Where's Will?' I blurt. I have to know.

Xander jerks a thumb to one of the nearby cars. 'Passed out in the back.' I squint through the gloom and notice a figure slumped in the back of a car. *Will*. So close, but he might as well be an ocean away. When last I saw him, he was promising to find me again. He was hurt, but conscious. I shudder to think what his own family may have done to change that.

'He needs a doctor,' I say.

'Later. After I deal with you two.'

'Look,' Cassian begins, stepping in front of me. 'I don't know what you think—'

'I *think* you need to shut up. I'm doing the talking here!' Xander grabs his shoulder. Big mistake.

Cassian growls, his skin flashing a glimmering charcoal. There's a flurry of movement and then Xander's on his back on the ground, his expression as stunned as the half dozen others gathered around us.

'Get him!' Xander shouts.

The others converge on Cassian. I scream, glimpsing Cassian's face amid the hunters. I cringe at the smacking sounds of fists and move toward them, determined to help him, but hands restrain me.

An animal growl rumbles on the air. It's Cassian. Several hunters hold him down. Angus grins as he plants a boot on his back. With his cheek pressed flat into asphalt, Cassian's gaze locks on me. His dark eyes shudder, the pupils thinning to vertical slits.

Steaming air rushes past my lips, but I suppress it and shake my head, conveying for him to hold off, to wait, still believing, hoping we can talk our way out of this. That he doesn't need to reveal himself as a draki, too. Maybe I can still protect him. Maybe he can make it out of here with Mom and Tamra.

The cold kiss of a gun digs into my ribs and I freeze. Mom cries out and I raise a hand, stopping her from doing anything foolish to help me. 'Stay with Tamra, Mom. She needs you!'

Xander's dark gaze roves over me contemptuously. 'I know what the hell I saw. A freak with wings.'

It's a battle not to let the fear swallow me in a fiery wash—a shock that I don't shift into my draki skin right now.

'Jacinda,' Cassian shouts my name, renewing his struggles.

Xander keeps talking. 'Don't worry. I'm not going to kill you. It's just a tranq gun. We'll keep you alive and figure out what the hell you are.'

They're beating Cassian now as he fights to get free.

'Stop!' I shove past Xander, but Angus blocks me. I watch in anguish as they keep kicking him. 'Stop! Please, stop!' My heart twists. It's them or us.

Fire erupts in my contracting lungs and climbs up my windpipe.

I can't let them take us.

Before I can release the blazing breath, a sudden gust of cold swirls around me. An unnatural chill. I shiver against the swift change in temperature.

As I whirl around, my throat constricts at the sight of Tamra. She stands alone, Mom watching with wide eyes several feet behind her.

My sister's face is dead pale, her eyes not her own anymore. Not like mine. The ice-gray chills my heart. A vapor rolls off her like steam. Except it's cold. The frigid mist grows, swelling in an ever-expanding cloud around us.

She arches her body in a sinuous ripple, tearing at her blouse, ripping it in a fierce move with her hands. Hands that suddenly wink and glimmer with a lustrous pearly sheen.

I've only seen such color on one other soul. Another draki. Nidia: the shader of our pride. I watch as the roots of Tamra's hair turn a silvery white that bleeds through the rest of her hair.

The vapor intensifies, a chilling mist that reminds me of home, of the fog that covers the township in a cool blanket. Shielding us from intruders, from any who would hunt and destroy us; obscuring the minds of those who stumble into our sanctuary.

'Tamra!' I reach for her, but Cassian's there, free from his attackers, his strong arm pulling me back.

'Let her,' he says.

I glance at his face, recognize the deep, primal satisfaction gleaming in his eyes. He's . . . *glad*. Happy at what's happening. What *can't* be happening. Tamra's never manifested before. How can this happen now?

In the moment I look away, it's done. By the time I look back to Tamra, she has risen several feet off the ground. Her gossamer wings snap behind her, the jagged tips peeking above her silvery shoulders.

'Tamra.' I breathe, absorbing the sight of her, grappling with this new reality. My sister's a draki. After so long. After thinking we would never have this in common. More than that—she's a shader.

Her eerily calm gaze sweeps over all of us on the road. Like she knows precisely what to do. And I guess she does. It's instinct.

I can't move as I watch her, both beautiful and terrifying with her shimmery skin, her hair leached of all pigment. She lifts her slim arms. Mist rushes over us like fast-burning smoke. So thick I can scarcely see my own hand before my face. The hunters are completely hidden, but I hear them as they holler and shout, bumping into one another, coughing, dropping onto the road like so many dominoes. First one, then another and another. Then nothing.

I strain for a sound in the sudden tomblike silence as Tamra's fog does what it's supposed to do and shades, shades, shades . . . everything in its path, every human nearby. *Will.*

I break away from Cassian and fight desperately through the cooling vapor that clouds both air and mind. Hunters sprawl at my feet, lowered by Tamra's handiwork. I see nothing through the all-reaching mist; my arms swing wildly through the cold kiss of fog, groping, searching for the car where Will lies.

Then I see him slumped in the backseat of the car. The driver's door yawns open, letting in the fog. The smoky haze curls around his sleeping form almost tenderly. For a moment I can't move. Only stare, strangling on my own breath. Even bruised and battered, he's beautiful.

Then action fires my limbs. I pull open the back door and reach for him. My shaking fingers brush his face and smooth back the honey strands of hair from his forehead. Like silk against my hand.

I jerk as Cassian roars my name. 'Jacinda! We have to go! Now!'

And then he's found me, drags me away toward our car. His other hand grips Tamra. He thrusts her at Mom. Her sparkly new body lights the desert night, cutting us a path through the great billowing mist.

Soon it will fade, evaporate. When Tamra's gone. When we've escaped. *The mist will fade. And with it, so will the hunters' memories.*

I'd once suggested to Tamra that her talent just hadn't manifested yet. That she was simply a late bloomer. Even though I didn't believe it, I'd said it. To give her hope. Even though, deep down, like the rest of the pride, I thought she was a defunct draki. Instead she's one of the most rare and prized of our kind. Just like me.

Behind the wheel, Cassian guns the engine and then we're shooting down the highway. I look behind us through the rear window at the great cloud of white. Will's in there. My fingers dig against the seat cushion until I feel the worn fabric give and tear beneath the pressure. No, I can't think about him now—it hurts too much.

My gaze drifts, brushes over the pale version of my sister, and I have to look away. Alarmed at the sight of my own twin, now as foreign to me as this desert.

I inhale a deep, shuddery breath. We're going home, to mountains and mists and everything familiar. The one place it's safe to be me. I'm going back to the pride.

2

The shrouded township of our pride rises almost magically on the hazy evening air. The narrow dirt road opens wider amid the towering, mist-laced trees and there it lies. Cassian sighs beside me and the tightness in my chest eases a bit. *Home.*

At first it simply looks like an imposing tangle of vine and bramble, but on closer inspection you can see that it's actually a wall. Behind it, my world hides in safety. The only place I ever thought I could live. At least before Will.

A guard stands on duty at the arched entry. Nidia's mist flows in a thick vapor around him. I recognize Ludo at once. One of Severin's flunkies, an onyx draki that likes to flaunt his muscles. His eyes round when he sees us. Without a word, he takes off into the township.

A guard is a peculiar sight. Nidia's cottage is positioned at the entrance for a purpose—so she can mark the arrival and departure of anyone. We have her and the watchtowers. A guard is an added precaution, and I wonder at the reason. Did we do this? Did our unsanctioned departure trigger a hypervigilance in security?

Cassian parks in front of Nidia's cottage. She's already outside her door, waiting as if she sensed our arrival. And I guess she did. That's her job, after all.

She stands so serenely; her hands clasped at her waist. The thick rope of her silvery hair hangs over one shoulder. *Hair almost identical to Tamra's.* My gaze involuntarily swings to my sister in the backseat, now a shader, too. Mom touches a tendril of her hair as if checking to see that it's real. I've watched her do this several times now.

'You've come home to us,' Nidia murmurs as I step from the car. The smile on her lips fails to meet her eyes, and I recall the night we slipped away from the pride— her shadow at the window and my certainty that she had let us go, let us escape. 'I knew you would. Knew in order for you to stay, you would have to go so you could learn that this is where you belong.'

I soak up my surroundings, my skin savoring the wet air—and I guess she's right. My body thrums at the re-energizing feel of the earth beneath me. This is home. I scan the streets involuntarily for Az, eager to see my best friend, but nobody is out.

Mom wraps an arm protectively around Tamra as they emerge from the car. Nidia moves forward to assist. My sister can barely walk. Her feet skim the ground between them.

'So you finally decided to come around, eh?' Nidia strokes a lock of silvery hair back from Tamra's pale cheek. 'Thought it was just a matter of time. Twins are such a rarity among our kind—I knew Jacinda couldn't possess a talent and not you.'

Cassian gives my sister a measuring look, a girl that he—the entire pride—dismissed as worthless. I can only guess at his thoughts. Now, with one of the most powerful, coveted talents among our species, she represents the future security of the pride.

As though he feels my stare, Cassian looks at me. I shift my attention to the others and follow them inside.

Within the cottage, the familiar scents wash over me. The lingering aroma of sautéed fish mingles with the comforting smell of herbs drying by the kitchen window. An easy warmth curls through me, and I shake off the sensation, reminding myself that this is a strained homecoming. I still have Severin and the elders to face. When I left they were on the verge of ordering my wings clipped. That's not something I can forget.

'There now. Aren't you the chilly one? I remember the early days of my first manifest. I never thought I would feel warm again.' Nidia places a delicately veined hand against Tamra's brow. 'Let's get you some root tea. Fluids will help restore you. And rest.' She moves into the kitchen and pours the steaming fluid from a kettle into a mug.

'Restore me to the way I used to be?' Tamra rasps from the couch, her voice rusty from disuse. These words are the most she's said since we left Chaparral. I release a ragged breath, relieved to hear her talking again. Silly maybe, but my heart lifts, glad to hear that this part of her is unchanged at least.

Nidia holds the steaming mug to Tamra's lips. 'Is that what you want?'

Tamra's gaze darts to me, Cassian, and then Mom, her icy eyes wary. 'I don't know,' she whispers before taking a sip from the mug and wincing.

'Too hot?' Nidia waves her hand over the mug, sending a cooling mist over the hot tea.

Mom lowers herself down beside Tamra, sitting close, almost as if she wishes to shelter her. Her gaze locks on Cassian. 'What now?' Her voice is defiant, as if he were the reason and not I that we're back. 'They'll be here any moment. What's going to happen? Will you see us punished?'

As the son of the pride's alpha, Cassian bears significant influence. He's next in line, primed to take control of the pride.

Sinking into a chair, I watch his face. Something flickers in his liquid, dark eyes. 'I promised Jacinda I would protect her. I would do the same for Tamra. And you.'

Mom laughs then. The sound rings hollow and dry. 'Thanks for throwing me in there, but I don't think for a moment you really care about me.'

'Mom—' I start to say but she cuts me off.

'And that's OK. As long as I have your word you'll keep Jacinda and Tamra safe. They're all I care about.'

'I give you my word. I'll do everything in my power to protect your daughters.'

She nods. 'I hope your word is enough.' Looking down again at Tamra, she seems full of regret, and I know she's mourning the loss of her one *human* daughter.

I shift, slide a hand under my thigh, and trap it between me and the seat, suddenly uncomfortable in the conviction that she mourns *me*, too. That she has for years.

It's a difficult thing, listening to my mother negotiate and plead for our safety—for mine. Because I screwed up. The memory of my final night with Will replays through my head. The pride has every right to be mad at me. I nearly killed us, all of us, everyone in the pride—and for a boy I'd known only a few weeks. If it wasn't for Tamra's shading, our secret would be in enemy hands—our greatest defense gone.

Cold washes up my back and slides over my scalp as a sudden realization presses down on me. *Will won't remember.* Even unconscious in the car, he was in close proximity to the mist. He would have been shaded. I desperately hope that some part of our last night together remains with him, enough so he knows I didn't just vanish from his life. He has to remember why I left. He must.

I'm still shaking, battling the idea that Will won't know what happened to me, when the elders arrive, walking into Nidia's little house without knocking. They fill the living room, overcrowding the small space with their towering forms.

'You've returned,' Severin declares, and I start at the deep sound of his voice even though I expected it.

Ever since we fled Chaparral, I've been hearing it in my head, imagining his voice ringing in my ears as he sentences me to a wing-clipping for my crimes. It's with dull acceptance that I face him.

Several elders loom behind Severin, their postures alike in their rigidity. They wear nothing special to mark their status. Their inherent bearing, the features schooled into impassivity, identifies them. I can't recall a time when I didn't know how to pick out an elder from the rest of us.

Severin scans us in one broad sweep and his gaze comes to rest on Tamra. His eyes flicker, the barest movement, the only outward sign he gives that he's surprised by her changed appearance. He examines her, missing nothing. Not the s lvery gray eyes. Not the shock of pearlescent hair. It's the same way he's looked at me for so long. I'm seized with the mad impulse to move between them, to block her from his drilling gaze.

'Tamra.' He breathes her name as though he were tasting it for the first time. He steps near to rest a hand on her shoulder. I stare at his hand upon my sister and something churns in my stomach. 'You've manifested. How wonderful.'

'So I guess she matters to you now.' It's too late to take the defiant words back. They rip from my lips with the speed of gunfire.

Severin glares at me. His eyes cold, dark pools of night. 'Everything—everyone—in this pride matters to me, Jacinda.' His possessive hand still lingers on Tamra as he says this, and I want to wrench it off her.

Yeah. Some of us just matter more.

'It's very unfair of you to imply differently,' he adds.

I resist the urge to press close to Cassian, hating to appear intimidated as his dad stares me down. I hold my ground and keep my eyes locked on Severin. My heart aches, a twisting mass in my chest. I've betrayed my kind. I've lost Will. Let them do their worst.

A corner of Severin's mouth curves upward with slow menace. 'It's good to have you back, Jacinda.'

3

I'm taken to my old house like a prisoner. Elders lead the way and follow at my back. It doesn't seem to matter that I returned voluntarily. Cassian made a point to tell them this. He said it more than once. But it only matters that I left, that I had the nerve to slip away—a precious commodity who dared to flee when the pride has specific plans for me.

Stepping inside my childhood home—it feels strange. The space seems smaller, more confining, and I become angry at myself. This house had been enough before. I inhale the stale air. No one has probably been here since we snuck away in the dead of night.

I stare at the couch, at the center cushion with its permanent indentation. It's Tamra's spot, her sanctuary. Shunned by the pride as a defunct draki, she'd lose herself for hours in front of the television. It feels wrong without her here, but I understand that it has to be this way for now. Severin commanded Tamra to remain with Nidia. Mom didn't argue, and I know it's because she thought another shader would know best how to care for Tamra during her adjustment to her talent.

'Are you going to tuck us in, too?' Mom snaps at the elders lingering inside our house. The faces that had been so familiar and harmless to me growing up watch me with condemnation.

Slowly, they turn and exit.

'Did you see Cassian walk off with Severin?' Mom asks, hurrying to the window. I nod as she parts the curtain. 'Hopefully, he'll persuade him not to . . . punish us too harshly for leaving.'

'Yeah.' Recalling Severin's delight over Tamra, I think it's a distinct possibility he'll be lenient with us.

With a grunt, Mom lets the curtain drop back in place. 'Two of them are still out there.'

I look out the window and spy the two elders standing on our front porch. 'They don't look like they're leaving any time soon. Guess they want to make sure we don't sneak away again.'

'Tamra's with Nidia.' Mom says this as if it's reason enough for us to stay put. And it is. Even if I wanted to leave the pride, I would never go without my sister. Especially now. My chest feels suddenly tight at the thought of what she must be going through. She must be so confused, so . . . lost.

'I'd never leave here without Tamra,' Mom says, echoing my thoughts. Her heated gaze shoots to me like I implied we should.

I look away, down at my hands, back out the window, anywhere but at her. I don't want her to see that I hear that *other* thing she's not saying. That I understand what her angry gaze tells me. *But I would leave without you.*

Maybe I'm not being fair. Maybe it's my guilt and she doesn't think that way at all.

Mom sighs, and I look back at her, watch as she tugs her hands through her hair. There are some gray strands in the curly mass. A first. 'I can't believe we're back here,' she mutters. 'Right where we started. Worse off than before.'

I cringe, feel this is a strike against me. Because it's my fault we're home again. All of this is my fault. I know that. And so does she.

'I'm tired,' I say. Not a lie. I don't think I've slept since leaving Chaparral, my thoughts too twisted up in everything that's happened. In all my colossal mistakes. In Will—wondering where he is, what he's doing, thinking, remembering. Or rather, failing to remember.

I move toward my room, feeling older than I've ever felt.

'Jacinda.'

I stop and look over my shoulder at the sound of my name. Mom's face is indecipherable, cast in shadow. 'Are you . . .' I hear her take a breath before she continues. 'That boy. Will—'

'What about him?' Even if Will is the last thing I want to talk about right now, I owe her answers. Even if it means prodding a fresh wound.

'Are you going to be able to forget him?' The ring of hope in her voice is unmistakable.

My thoughts drift back to Big Rock. To the sight of Will sliding down the rocky slope, straight into the grasping, waiting night. There had been no choice. I had to manifest. Had to save him. Even if hunters witnessed me doing it.

I had no choice then. And I have no choice now. 'I have to forget,' I reply.

Mom's amber gaze glows with knowing. 'But can you?'

This time I don't answer. Because words mean nothing. I'll have to show her, prove to her that she can trust me again. Prove to everyone.

Turning, I head toward my room, passing framed photos of the family we once were. Complete with a handsome father and smiling mother and two happy sisters who never knew how different they would be. How could we have known the reality that awaited us?

Kicking off my shoes, I change into an old T-shirt and shorts from my dresser drawer. My eyes barely glimpse the glowing stars dotting the ceiling before my lids drift shut.

It seems only minutes later that someone is shaking me, ripping me from the comforting embrace of sleep.

'Jacinda! Wake up!'

I shove a pillow off my head and peek blearily up at Az. Thrilled as I am to see her, I would rather pull the pillow back over my head and sink back into sleep, where guilt and heartache can't touch me.

'Az.' I rub a sleep-crusted corner of my eye. 'How'd you get in here?'

'My uncle Kel is on duty on your front porch. He let me in.'

That's right. Az's uncle was one of the elders staring at me like I was some sort of criminal. And I guess I am. In effect. I am under house arrest, after all.

'Good to see you,' I mumble tiredly.

'Good to see you?' She whacks me with a pillow. 'Is that all you can say after bailing and leaving me here alone while you run off to who knows where?'

'Mom was kind of insistent.' Now wasn't the time to explain why we left—what the pride had intended for me. Maybe still did.

Then I remember Az was with me that morning I nearly got captured by Will and his family. We both broke sacred rules sneaking off grounds to fly in the daylight. I sit up, stare at her with concern, looking her over. 'You didn't get in trouble, did you? For sneaking off grounds with me?'

Az rolls her eyes. 'They hardly spared me a thought after waking up to find you gone. Other than grilling me, that is.'

I exhale and drop back on the bed, relieved. At least I don't have that on my conscience, too.

Az shoves a long hank of blue-streaked black hair over her shoulder and leans above me, her eyes bright with emotion. 'You have no idea what it's been like since you left. *Because* you left!'

I roll over and hug a pillow. 'I'm sorry, Az.' Apparently, my conscience wasn't to be totally spared. Admittedly, I'd thought little of Az while I was away. I'd had enough to worry about trying to get through every day in Chaparral.

A tired sigh wells up inside me. Apologizing seems to be all I do lately.

Az sniffs. 'Well, at least you're home. Maybe things can go back to normal now.'

I think of Will and how I betrayed my own kind for him, of my sister and how lost she must feel, of the elders standing guard on my porch. I doubt if anything will ever be normal again. And yet, for all of that, I am relieved to be where my draki can thrive.

'It's been really suckish around here. Severin imposed a curfew. And he's tightened the leash on our rec time! Can you believe it? We're permitted to play airball once a week. *Once!* It's just school and work, school and work. He's a dictator!'

All this because of me? Because Mom took us and ran? Were they worried that others would do the same?

'At least we still get to fly,' she mutters. 'Don't know what I'd do without that. Scheduled group flight of course, though. That hasn't changed. But he's limited our air time.'

'Have you seen Cassian?' I ask.

Az arches an elegant eyebrow. 'Since when are you keeping tabs on him?'

'Since he's the one who found us and brought us back.'

'*Cassian* tracked you down? That's where he's been all this time? The word going around was that he took his tour.' She chuckles lightly. 'Man, oh, man, he's still got it bad for you.'

'Not *me*,' I quickly correct. 'He hasn't got it bad for me. 'If? he ever even wanted me—'

'If?'

I glare at her and continue, '*If* he even wants me it's only because I'm the pride's fire-breather.' A commodity, the pride's great weapon.

But then, not anymore. That's changed. Now there's Tamra. Tamra, who has always pined for Cassian. Maybe he'll finally return those feelings. Hope swells in my chest at the possibility. And some other emotion. Something I can't identify. Something I've never felt before.

'Whatever the reason, every girl in this pride would kill to have Cassian look at her the way he looks at you.'

22

She pulls a face and flips onto her back on my bed. 'Maybe even me.'

'You?' I blink.

'Yeah. Don't worry. This isn't a guilt trip. I never really thought I had a shot. No one did.' She winks at me. 'Not with you around.'

I groan. She sounds too much like Tam. The old Tamra. The one who longed for Cassian's attention and the pride's acceptance. The one who watched from the sidelines as I got both. Until we moved to Chaparral and she found a new life there. Which I took from her the night I dived off a cliff after a draki hunter.

Az glances around as if she'd heard my thoughts. 'Where's Tamra?'

'You mean you haven't heard?'

'Heard what?'

'She's with Nidia.' My lips twist into a smile even as my stomach gives a sickening lurch at the upheaval sure to come now that my sister's on her way to becoming the pride's next shader. 'Recuperating.'

'Recuperating from what?'

'Tamra manifested. She's a shader.'

Az's eyes round. 'No way!' She whistles through her teeth and tugs on her lip. 'Guess you're not the only prize around here anymore then.'

'Guess not,' I murmur, suddenly not sure whether this is a good thing or bad. I used to want to be a typical draki. Nothing extraordinary. Not the pride's great fire-breather under constant scrutiny and pressure. Now I appreciate that my uniqueness might be the only thing keeping me safe. But I also know Tamra's newfound talent means the pride will clutch both of us all the more tightly.

Az continues, 'Wonder whether Cassian will give her a second glance now.'

The floor creaks, alerting me to someone else's presence. I look up, my face growing hot that Mom may have overheard our conversation.

Only it's not Mom. It's worse.

The heat descends to my neck. 'How'd you get in here?' I demand, knowing Mom wouldn't have let him waltz into my room. At least not without warning me.

Cassian looks at me intently, his eyes more black than purple right then. The purple only shows itself when he's feeling emotion. A rarity it seems.

'How did you get in here?' I repeat. And then I realize it's a dumb question. He's one of them. One of my captors. The future leader of this pride, the *prince* can come and go as he pleases. 'Where's my mom?' I ask, straining for a glimpse beyond his large frame.

'Talking to my father.'

My skin shivers at this. Severin and my mom were never a good mix. I fight the urge to rush from the room, to find Mom and shield her. It's laughable really. Mom's the great protector—always looking out for me. Even when I don't want her to.

So I stay put, eager to hear whatever Cassian has come to say. At least I hope he'll tell me what's going on. What's going to happen to me. I'd rather hear it from him than Severin. Since Big Rock, we're in this together. I have to believe that.

He looks at Az pointedly, like he expects her to leave. So I can be alone with him? No thanks. I slide closer to her on the bed. His gaze narrows. Message received.

'Well? You talked with your dad. What's the verdict?' I draw a deep breath, ready to end the agony and find out

24

whether or not I have to endure a wing clipping. Does Severin know that I revealed myself to hunters? Did Cassian tell him that? My skin goes prickly hot at the very idea. No way Mom would volunteer *that* information.

'It's going to be OK, Jacinda.'

I angle my head. 'So I won't be punished?'

'I convinced them that you wanted to return. I told them you're eager to fall back into pride life. That you'll behave yourself and be more compliant.' His top lip curls faintly, and I remember what he told me back in Chaparral when he found me, that he liked me because I was different from everyone else here. Now he wants me to be the same.

I inhale sharply through my nose. *Compliant.* Submissive. Meek. Biddable. Do I even have it in me?

'Compliant? Jacinda?' Az giggles, unaware of the tension. 'They bought that?'

Cassian flicks her a hard glance, then looks back to me. Waiting. What? Does he expect to hear my agreement?

'Oh.' Az sobers, looking between our two serious expressions. 'Well, of course. I'm sure Jacinda will be more . . . I mean, I'm sure she realizes she belongs here. Your dad has to see that. Why would she want to stay out there—in a world she can never fit in?'

At my silence, Az swings me a questioning look. I wish I could explain to her that I might have found a reason to live out there among humans. It will take some convincing for Az to understand how I could have fallen for Will, and for whatever reason, I don't want to talk about it in front of Cassian.

The way Cassian's nostrils flare, it's not far from his thoughts anyway. Beneath the swarthy skin of his face, charcoal flashes—like a creature swimming beneath the water's surface. A beast I must placate.

I'm reminded of his animal strength, of his large frame colliding with Will on top of Big Rock. The unchecked violence as the two rolled in a twisting, tangled pile off the edge of that cliff—I shiver and press a hand to my stomach, a little sick at the memory. They wanted to kill each other. They almost did.

'You'll stay here with your mom,' Cassian announces when it becomes clear I'm not going to give him the agreement he seeks to be a meek and compliant little draki. It's not that I don't want to say the words. I'm simply afraid of promising something I *can't* do. 'You can start attending school again. And work. School, work, and home. Your sister will stay with Nidia.'

This gives me a start. I didn't think the separation would be permanent. I can't remember a time when Tam and I ever slept more than one room apart from each other. As much as this disturbs me, I guess it makes sense. Nidia will take care of Tamra. Give her the support and guidance she needs right now. Everything that Mom and I can't give her.

I tell myself that's all that's happening. The pride isn't trying to separate us.

'Tamra, a shader.' Az shakes her head, marveling. 'Wait until I tell everyone. This is awesome.' My friend squeezes my arm with happy enthusiasm. 'Hey, I gotta go.'

She hops from my bed, evidently eager to start spreading the news that our pride's future is assured. That we have a new shader who can take Nidia's place someday.

As long as Tamra doesn't mind being bound to the pride for the rest of her life. And why should she? Once

26

she has time to deal with the change, she's going to real-ize she's no longer invisible among the pride—and that she has a shot with Cassian.

Leaping through the door, Az calls over her shoulder, 'Be back later.'

And I'm alone with Cassian, after all. Thanks, Az.

4

We haven't been alone since Chaparral. On the journey here, the four of us trapped in the tight confines of the car, we hardly ever spoke, stopping only for gas, the rest-room, and the chance to grab some food. But now it's just the two of us.

I can only stare at him, dreading the torrent of admonitions I'm convinced he'll heap upon me. For the obvious reasons: exposing myself to our greatest enemy. Loving one of those enemies. And even worse, for *still* loving Will after seeing his blood. How can I explain to Cassian that Will's not the bad guy? He's just a victim of birth. The blood transfusions forced on him when he was sick. But then does it really matter that I explain anything? I'm not going to see him again.

In the silence I can hear the muffled voices of our parents. The tone is heated.

'What did you tell your father?' I slide off my bed, suddenly aware that I'm on my *bed* . . . that he's so close, looming right above me. He doesn't move, and I have to brush past him to get to the overstuffed sofa chair near the window.

'You mean did I tell them that you revealed yourself to humans?' His gaze cuts into me. 'To hunters?'

I fight back my cringe. It sounds even more awful when he says it. I wish I could deny it.

'Yeah. That.' Settling into the chair near my window, I try to act casual, unbothered at this reminder, unbothered about everything. Especially *him*. Here in my bedroom, staring at me in that consuming, searing way that makes my lungs pull and contract. 'Did you tell your father about that?'

That I did the one thing that could ruin us all. Not just the pride but our entire species.

His gaze sweeps me, missing nothing. Not the tangled mess of my hair trailing over my shoulders. Not my bare feet, peeking out beneath my folded legs. If he told them what happened, if he told them everything, how could they *not* punish me? Even a part of me believes I deserve it. I betrayed my kind.

Not that I would change anything I did even if I could. I know this much. It's a strange realization. Feeling guilty does not mean I regret anything. Stronger than any guilt I feel is the pain in my heart at losing Will. I can't imagine what that pain would be like if I hadn't saved him. If he'd actually died out there in the desert.

Finally, Cassian answers me. 'I couldn't keep it from them, Jacinda. Not that. It affects all of us.'

I sink down a little in the cushions. Almost like I'm disappointed in him. I don't know why. Despite our past friendship, I expect no loyalty from him. The pride is first and foremost with Cassian. Still, Tamra shaded the hunt-

29

ers. They won't remember. Couldn't he have kept it a secret? Would it have been such a bad thing to do?

Bleakness washes over me, slides through me like ice water. I had almost believed that he cared about me, that he would protect me. Like he promised. Instead, he threw me to the wolves.

'I had to tell them you revealed yourself to hunters, but I didn't tell them everything. I didn't tell them about *him*.'

I stare coolly; say the word he cannot bring himself to utter. 'You mean Will?'

Something passes over his face. For a second his pupils shudder, shrink, flash to the barest slits. Then nothing. He's the ever-stoic Cassian again. 'Yeah. I didn't tell them about the blood.'

That injects me with a shot of helpless shame. *Will's blood*. The blood that's the same color as mine. I nod.

'They would hunt him down if they knew. I guess I owe you for that.'

'You're not in love with him,' he says so suddenly and with such force that I jerk. 'You don't even know him. He doesn't know you. Not like I do.' His chest rises and falls with serrated breaths.

I say nothing in the awkward silence that follows. Tension swirls around us, as dense as Nidia's mists pressing at my window. I stare down at my hands, noticing the tiny half moons my nails dug without my even knowing.

He releases a heavy sigh. 'Look at me, Jacinda. Say something.'

I force my gaze back on him. Does he expect me to agree that I don't love Will? Determined not to discuss my feelings for Will, I say, 'Tamra shaded them. Why did you have to tell them anything? They look at me like I'm a criminal.' I wave an arm. 'I'm practically under house arrest! They're never going to forgive me.'

'I had to tell them. What if any of those hunters ever remember? Tamra doesn't know how to use her powers yet. What if it doesn't last? What if she didn't shade them enough?'

I nod, the motion somehow painful, nearly as painful as the tightness in my chest. 'I understand. It's fine.'

'Clearly, it's not fine. You're upset.'

I press a hand to my chest. 'And wouldn't you be, Cassian? I'm going to be treated like a traitor for the rest of my life.'

He shakes his head slowly, a muscle feathering the flesh of his clenched jaw. 'They'll forget and forgive. Eventually.'

'You can't know that.'

He'd said he would try to do everything he could to keep me safe, but even I know he's not in total control here.

'The fact that Tamra's here, that she's a shader, has greatly appeased them. That you're *both* back has.'

Even after he told them what I did? I stare at him doubtfully, afraid to drop my guard. 'So I'm not in trouble?'

'I didn't say that.' Something loosens in his face as he says this. A hint of a smile plays on his mouth. 'You did reveal yourself to a human, Jacinda. And his family of hunters.'

And for that, I must pay. I nod, accepting it.

'You've got a lot to make up for,' he adds, fully serious again.

31

'And if I can't?' I'm not sure I have it in me to prove my-self to anyone anymore. Right now, the thought of never seeing Will again tears through me and makes me feel bruised and tired. Even though a part of me is relieved to be back in the pride, I'm not exactly in the best condition to properly suck up to anyone.

'Then things will be hard for you. Harder than they have to be. And your mother . . .' His voice fades, but the threat hangs.

My eyes narrow, skin tightening and prickling. 'What about my mother?'

He glances over his shoulder as if he could see her wherever she stands in the house. 'There's no love for her. They blame her for taking you and Tamra. There's talk of banishment—'

I inhale sharply. 'That's not fair. I'm the one—'

'She took you away. You didn't leave on your own. Come on, Jacinda. Would any of this have happened without your mother hauling you off to some desert?'

I swallow thickly and look back out the window. I hate that I can't argue this point with him. Hate that I see his logic, as cruel as it is.

'None of us is an island. Think about that. The actions of one affect all.'

I guess this is how I'm not like the rest of them. Why I'm the one who has endangered us all.

I lightly brush my mouth, speaking through my fingers. 'Don't you get sick of it? Don't you ever want what *you* want? Don't you think you deserve that once in a while? Why must you put the pride first above every-thing? Above the life of one? Do you ever draw a line? You can rationalize the sacrifice of one, but what about when it's two? Three? When do you say enough?' I shake my head.

Cassian stares at me. 'It's the way we are. It's how we've survived this long. The fact that you even question it when no one else does—' He cocks his head to the side. 'But then maybe that's what makes you so special. Why I'm even here talking to you. Why I care at all.'

I swallow against the tightness in my throat and hold his stare. 'So you'—I struggle for the right word, a word that won't make my face heat unbearably, and settle on— 'you *like* me because I'm the kind of person that puts us all in jeopardy?'

That rare smile plays about his lips again. 'You're not dull, that's for sure.'

'Cassian.'

My nerves snap tight as Severin himself steps inside the room beside Cassian. The two of them . . . in my room. Not something I ever envisioned. Cassian is one thing. Severin, another.

Mom hangs back behind Severin, her face hard with defiance. I guess whatever they discussed did not sit well with her.

'We're finished here, Cassian.'

Severin's gaze rests on me. I feel myself shrinking inwardly. But I don't show it. I force myself to hold his stare, pretending he doesn't make feel weak and shaky inside, that I don't deserve censure.

Severin waves Cassian to the door. 'Wait for me outside.'

Cassian sends me a lingering look and then departs.

Mom moves more fully into the room, her thin arms crossed over her chest. She's lost weight. I wonder how I could have missed this. She always had curves before.

Severin looks at her coldly. 'I would like to have a word with Jacinda.'

'Then you'll have to do it in front of me.'

Severin's lip curls up over his bone-white teeth. 'You've already proven yourself a mother of dubious parenting, Zara. No need to behave as though you care for your daughter now.'

A stricken look flashes over my mother's face before she manages to mask it, but the paleness is still there, making her eyes stand out like giant gleaming pools.

Since Dad was killed, Tamra and I are all she has. Every decision she makes is in our best interest . . . in what she *thinks* is our best interest. She might have made a few mistakes, but I never doubt her love for me.

A quick simmer froths to life at my core. 'Don't talk to my mother that way,' I warn.

Severin looks back at me, *down* at me, as though I were something soiled at his feet. 'Have a care, Jacinda. You are pardoned for your offenses. A fact you can thank Cassian for. I'd just as soon see you punished—' He looks at Mom again. 'And you banished.'

'Don't do me any favors,' I snap, unable to strike the proper chord of penitence with Severin.

'Jacinda,' Mom says in a low voice, grasping my arm with cool fingers.

Severin's features harden. 'Heed me well. You're on thin ice, Jacinda. I expect perfect behavior from you from now on . . .' His voice trails, the threat deliberate, implicit. I practically hear him say, *Or else we'll clip your wings*.

I refuse to show that he affects me—that the threat works, sending a bolt of fear through me that makes

34

my skin tighten and the heat shiver beneath my flesh, a writhing serpent seeking release.

'She won't be any trouble,' Mom says in a voice I've never heard her use. She sounds almost beaten.

Severin's mouth curls in a smug smile. 'Maybe this time you'll do a better job of keeping her in line.' With a crisp nod, he leaves, his tread a thudding retreat from our home.

A home that no longer feels like home. Just a house that is not ours anymore. Not if Severin can march inside and issue commands and threats as if it were his right to do so.

For the first time I ask myself whether this is what the pride has become—or whether it has always been this way?

5

For a moment, we stand in silence, and then Mom settles down on my bed with a weariness that stabs at my heart. It's been too long since she last manifested—*years*. She's starting to feel her age.

She picks up the tattered bear Dad gave me on my seventh birthday from the tangle of sheets and pillows. I'd forgotten it when we left in such haste, and now I'm glad I left it. Glad that something loved and familiar is waiting for me here.

Mom plucks at one matted ear with a muted sigh. There's such defeat in the sound. In the sudden slump to her shoulders. Is this it then? Has she given up?

At last she speaks, and her voice is as hollow and flat as her eyes. 'I want you safe, Jacinda. I don't want you hurt.'

I nod. 'I know.'

'And right now I'm starting to think I might be the one causing you the most suffering.'

I shake my head fiercely, not liking this new, defeated

version of my mother. She's someone I don't know. Don't want to know. With everything else changing, I need her to remain constant. 'No. That's not true.'

'I've shoved and pushed you every which way whether you liked it or not—all with the goal of protecting you.' She shakes her head. 'Maybe I've made everything worse. Now we're back here.' She motions listlessly with her hand. 'You're just as much a slave to the pride. Only this time it's worse. They'll no longer treat you like you're a great gift bestowed upon them. They'll treat you like you're some kind of malcontent.'

'Mom?' My voice quavers a bit and I swallow. 'What are you saying?'

She looks up from the bear. 'Don't let them treat you like a whipped dog for the rest of your life. Follow their rules. Lay low. Get back on top. Do what you have to.'

'You actually want to stay here? You want Tamra to stay here?'

'Taking you to Chaparral . . . I was chasing a dream. Something that never existed. Not for you or even Tamra. She was destined to be a draki and I didn't even know it.' She strangles on a laugh, presses her fingers to her lips to catch it. 'And you—well, you've been trying to tell me all along that you can't be anything but a draki. That you need to be here. I just didn't want to hear it. I'm sorry, Jacinda.'

I sit down beside my mother on the bed. She might have infuriated me in the past, but I can't stand seeing her like this. I want her back. I miss her vibrancy. Miss her. 'Don't be sorry. Don't ever be sorry for being a mother who loves her daughters so completely she would sacrifice everything for them.'

I hold her hand, squeeze the cold fingers, and suddenly remember that she's always cold here. Always shivering in the perpetual mists and winds. The same mist and wind that are home to me—that I lift my face to better feel and taste. She didn't love it. Never had and never will. 'We'll figure out a way to live here. Happily. I'm not going to live with my head bowed and neither will you.'

She gives me a wobbly smile and reminds me gently, 'Your sister's head isn't bowed here anymore.'

That's true. Tamra's on top now. And ironically, I'm not. At least not at the moment.

Mom brushes my cheek with the back of her hand. 'I lived here for your father. I can do it for my girls. It's a small price to pay.' She sucks in a breath. 'I loved your dad very much. But that love was nothing like how I felt after we were bonded. Something happens, changes when you're bonded in that circle. It's like we became connected . . .' Her expression grows wistful. 'Some days, I couldn't tell my emotions from his.' Her amber gaze darkens. 'Even that last day . . . I felt . . . I knew something was wrong before anyone told me. And I stayed here for so long, telling myself that the *nothingness* I felt wasn't him dead. That he could still be alive out there, just out of my range so I couldn't sense him anymore.'

I watch her raptly. 'Why did you never tell me this?' At least the part about feeling something was wrong with Dad that last day. Of course I knew that many bonded draki form a connection. Historically, dragons mated for life and the idea behind bonding stems from this ancient trait. For some draki couples it goes deeper. Apparently my parents had been one of them.

She shrugs. 'You were just a girl. I didn't want you to know that I'd felt his . . . fear. His pain. I nearly passed out from it, Jacinda. I was afraid if I told you, you would think I'd felt his . . .'

'Death,' I supply. My head aches, temples throbbing as I process this. Deep in my soul, I held hope that Dad lived. That he could be in captivity somewhere. I don't know what to think anymore.

She flinches but nods.

'So why are you telling me now?' I demand. Mom had practically been in Dad's head at the end . . . and she kept that to herself?

'You need to know.' She tucks a strand of hair behind my ear. 'In case you ever bond with someone here.' My eyes widen, already guessing the direction she's heading. And not believing it. She can't be *suggesting* I bond with Cassian. 'You'll feel . . .'

'What?'

She fixes her gaze on me. 'It'll be OK, Jacinda.'

OK? 'Because once we're bonded it won't matter that I don't love him? Because I'll feel something false and can lie to myself that it's love?'

She shakes her head firmly. 'You'll feel connected. Once that happens, does it really matter why or how it happened?'

Yes!

'It mattered to you before,' I say numbly.

'Things are different now. We're stuck here. You need to make the best of it.'

'I am. I will. That doesn't mean I have to get myself bonded.' I close my eyes and rub my eyelids, trying to ease the ache there. Am I really having a conversation with my mother on the pros of bonding in order to escape the pride's disapproval?

'You can be happy here, can't you? Cassian—' She stops. I watch her throat work, incredulous over what she's saying. 'Cassian's not a bad sort. He's not . . . quite like his father.'

Not quite. I pull back, certain my mother has been snatched up by aliens. 'Are you serious?'

'The pride would forget everything if you and Cassian just—'

'No! Mom, no!' I resist the temptation to cover my ears with my hands. I'm not hearing this. Not from her.

'I'm not saying right now. In time—'

'I can't believe you're saying this!'

She grips my hand, speaks to me in a hard voice. 'I can't protect you anymore, Jacinda. I've no power here.'

'And because Cassian does that's reason enough to barter myself?'

'I'm not suggesting anything you haven't considered already. I've seen you with him. There's something there.'

I nod slowly. 'Maybe. Once.' When there was no one else. No alternative to tempt me. Before I met Will. 'Not anymore.'

'Because of Will.' Mom's eyes spark for a moment with the old vitality. 'You can't be with him. It's impossible, Jacinda. There's no chance. He's not one of us.'

He's not one of us. I've avoided really thinking about that, accepting that, but the words find me now, dig deep and wound me where my heart already aches.

I inhale thinly. 'Impossible or not, I can't consider anyone else. I'd rather be alone.'

'Oh, don't be naïve! He's a human! A hunter! Let it go! There will be someone else.'

For a moment, the conversation strangely echoes when Mom tried to persuade me to let my draki go, let it wither away. Now she wants me to embrace my draki and forget Will. I shake my head.

Only she's right. More than she even realizes. Hanging on to Will is foolishness. It's wrong. I know this. He's more than an untouchable human. More than a hunter. He's much worse.

Draki blood runs through his veins. A draki—perhaps several—died in order to sustain his life. Even if his father was responsible for the terrible deed, how could I ever look Will in the eyes again? Touch him? Hold him? Kiss him?

I suppose it's a good thing I will never face him again. I need to quit hoping, in the darkest shadows of my heart, that he will keep his promise to find me.

'I've let him go,' I murmur, my voice soft.

Mom studies me, her expression unconvinced. But then I don't need to convince her as much as I need to convince myself.

That night in my bed, I stare at the glowing stars Dad helped me decorate the ceiling with years before and gradually begin to feel safe again. The way I felt as a little girl, my parents asleep just down the hall from me. So secure. So protected.

I free my thoughts and find Will. He's waiting there in my unguarded heart.

Dozing, half asleep, I remember. Remember him—us—those moments before the world crashed down around me. A smile touches my lips as I remember everything. I remember until the longing becomes too much. Until the ache of wanting him becomes too deep, as salty as the warm tears flowing down my cheeks.

It's not over. We're not through . . . I'll come for you. I'll find you. I will. We'll be together again.

'No,' I whisper into the hush of my room even as my heart bleeds. A treacherous part of me forever wants to believe that. 'We won't.'

But then I wake up to the horrible truth again, hiss at the sudden knifing pain to my heart. He won't have those memories. He won't remember making that promise to me.

I brush fingers to my trembling lips. *You won't remember me leaving. You won't remember why I had to go. You'll just think I left Chaparral. Left you.*

Turning my face, I bite my pillow, stifling the sob that wants to break loose from my chest.

Does he even think about me anymore? Desperately I wonder how much, how far back can he remember? How much of me is gone? Tamra is new at this. Could she have wiped me completely from his memory? I shake my head at the thought. Bite my lip until I taste the tang of my own blood. Releasing the bruised flesh, I tell myself I'm being paranoid. I've never heard of a shader who could erase weeks from a person's mind. It isn't possible. It can't be.

In that moment, I know. I have to ask Tamra. I have to find out if she knows how much memory she took from Will. How much of me she erased from his heart.

Rolling to my side, I feel a small measure of comfort. Tomorrow. I'll ask her tomorrow.

Somehow this decision makes me feel better. Gives me something to look forward to even though nothing she says will change anything.

Will is miles away in Chaparral. And I'll still be here.

When I step out on our porch the following morning, I release a deep breath of relief, glad to see our watchdogs have been called off. I guess Severin decided yesterday's chat was enough to keep me in line.

It's still early. A thick fog clings low to the ground, hugging my calves and rising up in a thinner mist as I set out for Nidia's cottage, determined to ask Tamra if she thinks she succeeded in shading Will and the others. It was her first time, after all. How can she be sure she knew what she was doing?

Jabel's dog barks. I quicken my pace, imagining I see the blinds shift. I don't want to get stuck talking to Cassian's aunt. I look over my shoulder, wondering if she's the reason Severin sent our bodyguards home. It's convenient, after all, to have the watchful eyes of his sister across the street from us.

I should have been looking where I was going. A cry escapes me as I collide hard with another body.

Hands reach out and steady me. I blow messy hair from my face and gaze upon Corbin, Jabel's son.

'Jacinda,' he greets. 'Nice to have you back.' His mouth lifts in a smile that doesn't seem real, but then it never has.

Corbin and I are the same age—we've been in the same classes since primary school. But we were never close. He was always mean-spirited, cheating at school and games. Playing cruel pranks on those smaller. When it became clear I was a fire-breather, he'd suddenly changed his tune and tried cozying up to me, but by then I knew the real Corbin.

He resembles his uncle Severin. Much more than Cassian does. It's the eyes. Corbin and Severin possess the same dead eyes. If possible, he's grown in my absence. He stands almost as tall as Cassian now. I step from the clasp of his hands and try not to appear intimidated.

'Where you headed?' he asks.

I bristle, thinking how his mom is probably spying on us as we stand here. How he was probably lying in wait for me to leave my house. 'Why? Have you been assigned to guard me?'

He gives me what I guess is a flirty smile. 'Do you need a bodyguard?'

I shake my head, regretting my defensiveness. If I act like a prisoner, that's how they'll treat me. 'I'm going to see my sister.' *To satisfy my morbid fear that Will doesn't remember our last night together. That as far as he's concerned, I simply vanished.*

'Oh.' He digs his hands deep into his pockets. 'I'll walk with you.'

Not seeing how I can refuse this, I give a light shrug and continue on, the mist weaving around my ankles. We walk past houses with their windows drawn against the morning. I don't remember the pride being this quiet before, this still. Even this early, there was usually some activity. It gives me an eerie feeling. Suddenly the vine-covered wall edging the township doesn't seem like something protecting us, but something hemming us in.

'So quiet,' I murmur.

'Yeah. Still curfew. You can't leave your house until seven.'

'Then what are you doing wandering—'

'I'm part of the morning patrol.' He gestures to the blue band around his arm. I hadn't noticed it before.

'Patrol,' I echo numbly, staring at the blue fabric. 'I didn't know. Should I go back until—'

'Nah. I won't write you up.' *Write me up?*

He smiles like this is a gift. I can't muster a smile in return. I want no gifts from him. Tomorrow I'll be certain to leave *after* seven.

I turn and continue walking.

'Pretty cool about your sister,' he says, keeping pace with me.

'Yeah.'

He slants me a look from his night-black eyes. 'You don't sound happy about it.'

'Honestly, I haven't had time to process it.'

He nods like he understands that. 'It will be a huge adjustment.'

'Yes. Nidia will help Tamra get through it all—'

'I meant an adjustment for you,' he smoothly inserts, his voice as slick as oil.

The pulse at my neck skitters erratically. 'Me?'

His shoes scrape loose gravel on the path. The sound frays my nerves. 'Yeah. You're not top dog around here anymore.'

I quicken my pace through the town center, past the school and meeting hall, eager to reach Nidia's. 'It was never like that.'

'Yeah, it was. But now there's two of you. You've got some competition.'

I stop and face him even as a part of me just wants to walk faster and leave him far behind. That or punch him.

45

He arches a golden eyebrow. 'I'm just saying.' He waves a hand. 'Cassian can't have *both* of you.'

I stare hard at him. He doesn't flinch. Doesn't even look away.

I cross my arms over my chest and decide to get to the point. 'Meaning *you* have a shot at one of us now?'

He smiles that non-smile again, and I suddenly loathe him—this grasping, greedy boy that sees me or my sister as a way to climb the ranks. I despise that he thinks he can possess whoever Cassian doesn't want. Because it's as simple as Cassian choosing. And Corbin taking, seizing the leftovers like any foraging dog. My muscles tense in anger. *Like hell.*

I snort and turn, start walking again, my steps faster, hard nips into the ground. 'It's not going to happen,' I toss over my shoulder.

'You can't run from it, Jacinda. Not anymore.'

'From what?' I whirl around, wanting to be perfectly clear on whatever he's implying.

'If you don't pair up with Cassian, my uncle will look to me next. We could be good together, Jacinda.'

'You've got to be kidding.'

His chest swells with self-importance. 'My bloodline has led this pride for the last four centuries. Even your father could not usurp my family's power.'

'What do you know about my father?' I charge forward.

'Just what I've been told. Before he disappeared, he was constantly challenging my uncle. To no avail. My family is the best suited to rule this pride. We've always been the strongest . . . and we'll only grow stronger with a fire-breather and a shader added to our line.'

I feel my face grow clammy-cold at the thought of *Corbin* and *me*, and I admit to myself that the idea of Cassian never made me feel this ill.

'You're nuts.' I continue walking, relief flooding me when he doesn't follow.

'You don't get to decide anymore, Jacinda!' he calls after me. 'You lost that chance. It's going to be me or Cassian.'

I know this is not an idle threat. He's Severin's favored nephew, after all. He would know things. Things I wouldn't. And unlike Cassian, he's not trying to help me behind the scenes.

I tell myself to be glad he told me his plans. Now I can work to make certain that they don't happen. Tamra and I aren't going to be bullied into bonding with anyone. Unless we want to, of course. I wince, thinking that Tamra would most definitely want to bond with Cassian.

Corbin's voice follows me through the mist. 'Tell Tamra I'll stop by later.'

And this makes me shiver.

I suppose I should want him to pair up with Tamra. To spare me from the awful prospect of him. But I wouldn't wish him on my worst enemy, much less my own sister.

I stride toward Nidia's with determined steps, working to convince myself that the pride isn't some fascist regime where its inhabitants suffer total subjugation. It isn't. It's the only place my draki can live in freedom. I slow as I approach the cottage, noticing a lone figure standing guard just inside the arched entry to the township. As I approach, I recognize Gil, a friend of Cassian's.

I wave at him in greeting.

'Going to see your sister?' he calls.

I nod, then frown at the goofy grin splitting his face. 'Tell her I said hi.'

'Hi,' I echo.

Gil had never paid any attention to my sister before. As far as I know, he's never even spoken to her before. He's one of the many who looked *through* her rather than at her. Now he wants me to pass along a hello?

Disgust washes through me. Just like it was with me, no one really cares about Tamra. They don't care about the girl, just the talent.

At my knock, Nidia answers the door. With a wave, she motions me inside her cottage that always smells of herbs and baking bread. My refuge so many times. Especially after Dad died. Now it's Tamra's refuge.

I step into the welcoming warmth. And stop cold.

I'm not the only one visiting this morning.

My sister lounges on the couch. A blanket is tucked around her and she holds a steaming mug in her hands. She no longer looks like my twin. Icy hair, red no more, flows past her shoulders. She still manages to coif it perfectly, better than I could ever fix my hair, and I wonder whether Nidia owns a flat iron. It's amazing how her new hair color changes everything about her. Even her face looks different, bears little resemblance to mine. Especially with those frosty gray eyes.

My gaze skips to her visitor, sitting so close, relaxed on a foot stool beside the couch. Cassian smiles at my sister in an easy, unguarded way. It's a smile he wore often when we were carefree children.

A small chill chases up my spine, sliding through my hair and rippling over my scalp. I hug myself like I'm seeking warmth, but it's something else, something more I need.

I stare at my sister beaming at Cassian and heaviness sinks to the pit of my stomach. In that second, I feel more alone than I've ever felt. I couldn't have missed Will more.

Will understood about loneliness. About being apart, separate from the world that you inhabit. A stranger among your own kind. Will understood that. He understood me.

6

Nidia's voice announces my arrival. 'So nice of you to visit, Jacinda. Would you like some hot chocolate?'

I nod and soon find myself settled into a chair with a mug in my hands. Tamra still wears a smile, but it looks brittle as she turns to me, waiting for me to speak. In those strange eyes lurks the same wariness I feel. We don't know what to say to each other or how to behave. We don't *know* each other anymore. I've only been guessing at how she feels over suddenly manifesting. I don't really know.

'Good to see you up,' I finally say, and then lie, 'You look well.'

'I'm feeling better,' Tamra offers in a voice that sounds friendly, but distant. I want to close that distance. Sit down next to her and remind her of what we are to each other. 'Nidia is taking excellent care of me.'

'We knew she would,' Cassian volunteers, and I want to strike him. *We?*

I bite back the stinging retort that we would have taken good care of her, too. Mom and me. We've always looked out for each other . . . except the pride won't let us anymore. I'm not sure who they consider the worse influence: me or Mom. I stare at the moonlight pale version of my sister and wonder whether she even wants to be with us. Does she miss us? Does she want to remain here?

'You look good, too, Jacinda,' Tamra adds, and I know she's lying. She's never been a fan of my T-shirt and jeans wardrobe. And the rest of me . . . I gave myself a cursory inspection as I brushed my teeth this morning. The shadows under my eyes looked like bruises, and even my lips seemed pale, colorless. Funny that I should look my worst here, in the cool mountains that have always revitalized me so much, in the mists and mountains I thought I needed to keep my draki alive.

'Thanks,' I say.

'I'm starting training tomorrow.' Tamra props herself up a little higher on the couch cushions. 'With Nidia and Keane.'

I nod. Keane is the pride's flight master. No draki takes to the sky without going through the ropes with him first.

'I bet you're looking forward to that.' And I smile, truly happy that she'll know what it's like to fly. She'll taste wind and sky and clouds. I know how wonderful it is and now so will she. We'll have that in common at last. She'll understand what I've been talking about all this time— she'll understand my need to keep my draki alive. It's a strange concept. I can hardly wrap my head around it as I stare at the stranger my sister has become. Tamra. Flying. Tamra finally understanding why I can't give it up. Why I can't let my draki wither away.

Nidia speaks then, and her words are like a surge of cold wind. 'I knew both of you were destined for great

51

things. You were such special children . . . and twins are so rare among our kind.'

My gaze swings to her as she lowers herself down on the window seat, picking up her discarded knitting. Needles *click clack* as she smiles and shakes her head, clearly pleased with herself. 'A fire-breather and a shader.' Beams of mote-filled light stream through the window at her back. Her silvery hair glints as if diamonds were buried in the dense mass.

'I still can't believe it,' Tamra marvels, looking dazed and a little giddy.

'Believe it,' Cassian says, squeezing her shoulder.

I stare at his large hand, his blunt-tipped fingers on her delicate shoulder, and I can't help wondering whether he's ever even touched her before. I know he hasn't in the last five years. I suppose he did before then. When we were children and you just liked who you liked and played games together.

Things were simple then. Before I manifested and Tamra didn't. Before she became a defunct draki in the eyes of the pride.

I draw a deep breath and tell myself that it's OK for him to touch her. It doesn't mean anything, and even if it did, even if Tamra ends up with Cassian, is that so bad? She'll get what—*who*—she's always wanted. I can't begrudge her that happiness. Not when she's had so little before now.

And it wouldn't mean I'd end up with Corbin. No matter what he said. I could still be the pride's fire-breather without bonding with someone. Corbin was wrong about that.

Moistening my lips, I say, 'I owe you a big thank-you, Tamra.'

She blinks her frosty eyes. 'For what?'

'For saving us back in Chaparral.' For saving me here, I think but don't say. Without *her*, the pride would probably have unleashed its full wrath on me.

'You're thanking me? That's unexpected. I didn't think you would appreciate me shading Will's memory.'

I inhale a shallow breath. 'You did what needed to be done. I know that.'

'Yeah. *I* did.'

I wince, certain she's implying that *I* didn't. I didn't do what I should have. I manifested before hunters to rescue Will. She wouldn't condone me ever doing that.

I glance uneasily at Nidia by the window. She focuses on her knitting, but I'm not so foolish to think she's not absorbing every word, spoken and unspoken.

As though she wants to make sure I catch her meaning, Tamra asks, 'But you didn't, did you? You didn't do what you should have.'

'Tamra,' Cassian says warningly. As though he's trying to protect me. From my own sister. The irony isn't lost on me that I spent years protecting Tamra from him. Even if he didn't know it, he hurt her constantly with his cold indifference.

'Stay out of this,' I growl.

'Cassian, come.' With a jerk of her head, Nidia rises and motions to the door.

Cassian nods. Together, they step outside, leaving us alone to talk.

I inch closer to the couch. 'I don't want to fight with you.'

Her features soften. 'Neither do I.'

'So,' I say lamely, sitting across from her. 'How's it going? How are you handling all of . . . this?'

53

'Pretty good.' She glances out the window at air that grows murkier with every moment. After a minute she looks back at me with her frosty gaze. 'Come with us tonight. We've never flown together. I want you there.'

'Sure,' I agree. Flying always revives my spirit, gives me strength. I could use that now. 'When does Nidia start training you?'

'Actually we've already begun,' she says with a laugh. 'Which is basically her talking a lot and giving an occasional demonstration. She says I'll get to try it again soon.'

I couldn't ask for a better lead-in.

'About that, how much damage do you think you did that night?'

She blinks those crystalline eyes, looking so otherworldly right then. Like those eyes are looking at me through some kind of veil while the real Tamra hides beneath, buried away.

'*Damage?*'

I wince. Too late, I realize I should have chosen a better word. A nicer word. Her talent is a gift. Each draki talent is a gift. That's what we're taught since primary school anyway. Even talents best geared to create harm. *Like fire-breathers.*

She's a shader. A draki that doesn't have to harm anyone to protect and save lives. I should be so lucky.

I quickly try to recover. 'I mean do you know the extent of'—I wave a hand—'of what you did that night?'

She looks at me intently with her ghost eyes, making me squirm.

'You cleared their memories, but do you know how far back you erased?' I pluck at the edge of a pillow. 'Do you have any idea—'

'This is about Will, isn't it?' She drags a hand through her silvery hair. 'You want to know how much of *you* I cleared from his memories, is that it?'

The sound of her voice is tinny in my ears and makes me nervous . . . like a wire that's about to snap and might catch me in the face. I shake my head, knowing instinctively that I don't want to hear whatever she's about to say. 'N-no—'

'You haven't let any of it go, have you?' she asks evenly, but the words feel as though she yells them. 'You're still hung up on him.'

'No,' I deny, but my voice sounds small and weak. Even I can't convince me. 'That's not true. I know I have to let him go, but it's not just a switch I can flip off. I wish it were.'

She sighs. 'I guess I can understand that. I pined long enough for someone I stood no chance of winning.' She means Cassian, of course. 'But you can't ever forget that he's a human. You can't keep going on loving a guy who hunts our kind.'

A sharp gasp rips the air behind me. Jumping to my feet, I spin, spotting Az and Miram, Cassian's sister, in the open doorway.

Nidia stands behind them, her expression shocked and regretful. 'Tamra, you have more . . . visitors,' she says lamely.

Cassian is there, too, towering over them all. The look in his eyes makes me feel foolish and pathetic. I take a long-suffering blink, wishing suddenly I'd told Az about Will rather than have her walk in on the truth like this. Opening my eyes again and seeing her face, I feel my stomach sink.

I make a move toward her.

'Is it true?' she demands, looking only at me. 'You fell for a hunter? One of those . . . *dogs* that chased us through the forest? Tried to kill us?'

I can see in her eyes that the memory still haunts her, and I know with a sick twist of my heart that she'll never believe that Will is anything but an animal.

'Please, Az. Let me explain. Will's not—'

'This is priceless,' Miram cuts in with relish.

'Miram,' Cassian rebukes his sister. She just shrugs.

Az drops the basket she's carrying. Fruit and muffins tumble to the floor as she turns and flees.

'Az,' I whisper, the look of betrayal on her face permanently etched in my mind. Another guilty memory.

Miram remains. With a grin spreading across her face, she's the most animated I've ever seen her. Visiocrypters don't show much emotion. They don't show much of anything. That's part of their nature. Bland, sandy-colored hair with eyes to match. They're nondescript, equipped to blend into the background.

'Oh, this is good,' she says. 'I can't wait to tell everyone.'

'Miram,' Cassian says sharply, but she's already gone.

She moves so fast, I'm not sure she didn't just fade out into invisibility.

Cassian moves to my side and looks down at me. 'I'll talk to her.'

For a moment, I let myself soak up his nearness and take comfort from the reassuring words. Then, I catch myself and give my head a small shake. Even if Cassian means that, I can't expect him to rein in his younger sister. Still, as I watch him take long strides out the door, I can't help hoping he can stop her from spreading what Cassian himself had tried to keep from the pride. For my sake. But I doubt he can.

Miram was never a fan of mine. Combine that with her love for gossip and this news is probably already half-way across the township. And she's a visiocrypter. She can make herself invisible and hide her very presence whenever the mood strikes. As much as I hate to stereotype, such draki are deceptive by nature.

What Cassian sought to spare me from is unavoidable. Everyone will know that the pride's fire-breather gave her heart to a hunter. I might be pardoned and spared a wing-clipping, but I'll never be forgiven, never be viewed as brethren again.

Panic surges in my chest as I listen to Cassian's tread fade away outside. I hurry to the door and look after him until he disappears into the misty morning.

Turning back around, I face Nidia's pitying stare. When did I become the pitiable one? That's something new. Evidently, I'm not to be envied anymore.

Tamra looks down into her mug, unable to meet my gaze. The nervous fidgeting of her hands tells me she's sorry she said what she did—that Az and Miram overheard.

'Hey.' I force my voice to sound normal, even cheerful. 'Don't look so sad.'

She lifts her gaze. Her eyes glisten like ice. 'I'm so sorry, Jacinda. For what I said . . . that they overheard . . .'

I move, drop down beside her on the couch and hug her. 'It's not your fault.' I stroke her back in soothing circles. 'None of this is your fault.'

The only person I can blame is me.

School in the pride is nothing like in the human world. We attend year-round, but never for a full day, and maybe only a few days a week depending on the course of study.

Everyone has duties and tasks to attend to in order for the pride to function. We grow various crops, leave lines in the mountain streams for fish, occasionally hunt for meat. We also repair and maintain our current structures, fence lines, and, of course, the outer wall is always cultivated to look indigenous to the wild terrain.

Even though we buy supplies from sporadic outings into the human world, the pride must be self-sufficient. Which is why, before my afternoon class, I head over to the library to do my part and resume my assigned duty.

The library detail is one of the most coveted assignments. It beats plowing a field or maintaining the pride's sewers.

The library sits beside the school. The two buildings are attached by a breezeway. The door gives a single, muted chime as I enter, eager to see the librarian, Taya, one of the oldest earth draki in the pride. She doesn't talk much, preferring the pages of a book to actual company, but we shared a sort of camaraderie from the years I'd been assigned as her assistant.

I've always found her a fount of information. She's not simply the pride's librarian. She serves as historian, too—responsible for recording all significant events in the pride's Great Book.

She looks up from this book as I enter, pen poised in one hand over the mammoth leather-toiled tome. A page flips without touch, landing as gently as the brush of a moth's wing.

She never has to actually touch the pages to turn them. As an earth draki, she has influence over any material originating from the earth. Since the pages of a book derive from trees, she pretty much doesn't have to handle anything directly in the library at all.

She squints as I approach, the only draki I know in need of spectacles. As draki have excellent vision, I'm certain it's a consequence of the centuries she's spent poring over texts by dim lighting.

'Jacinda,' she says hollowly, in a tone I've never heard from her before. Her features don't move, don't give the slightest flicker. She doesn't even rise to move around her desk. She is completely unmoved at the sight of me. And I know she knows . . . probably heard the whispers fluttering through the misted streets of the pride since yesterday.

I spent most of the day hiding, hoping against hope that Cassian was able to rein in his sister. Mom went out, though, and when she came back, I took one look at her grim face and knew that Miram's work was done.

'Hello, Taya.' I pause to deeply inhale the musty scent of books greeting me. 'I've missed this place.' An awkward silence hangs on the air. 'So.' I attempt a smile. 'What do you have for me to do today?'

Taya blinks. 'Didn't anyone tell you?'

'Tell me what?'

Her lips purse unhappily—not because of whatever news she has to impart but because *she's* the one who has to impart it. 'Your position has been filled.'

'Filled?' I echo.

'That's right.' She nods briskly.

Then I hear it. My heart sinks as a soft hum ripples through the quiet library. It's a bland, unremarkable tune, and I instantly know who it belongs to and who's about to round the corner.

Miram appears, carrying a stack of books. She stops when she sees me, her face revealing nothing. Naturally.

'What are you doing here?' Her lips, very nearly the same color as her strangely neutral skin, barely move.

'I work here. At least I thought I did.'

'You thought wrong. Lots of things have changed since you left.'

I'm beginning to see just how many.

Taya looks back and forth between Miram and me. This is probably more conversation than she gets in a week. With a faint smile and shrug of apology that lacks any real regret, she returns to her work.

Miram waves her fingers at me. 'Goodbye.'

Without a word, I turn and head out the door, walk past the school, ignoring the stares, the indiscreet whispers, and pointing fingers.

I'm almost to the meeting hall when something hits me in the head. I stagger, clutch my face, more stunned than hurt. It's a ball.

There's a burst of laughter, and a shouted taunt followed by children's feet scampering away. Heat flares through me, spreading from the inside out. It hadn't been an accident.

Tears burn and prick at my eyes, which makes me furious. I loathe this weakness—that I would crumble over a child's prank. I lean against the short stone wall edging the meeting hall, taking a moment to reclaim my composure. *I will not cry.*

It's hard sought. As the throbbing in my cheek really penetrates, really begins to smart, the steam builds in me.

Closing my eyes, I sip air, cooling my lungs. It's a dangerous feeling, this anger, this building fire inside me that wants to unleash itself. And not just because some kids hit me with a ball. It's everything. Az ignoring me.

Getting rebuffed by Taya . . . I always thought she liked me. I sniff and rub at my burning nose.

I should expect no less. It's no less than I deserve. These children playing in the streets—I put them in danger. I can't ever forget that.

Still, Will's face rises in my mind. His changeable eyes so clear, so tender as he gazes at me. I see him so well just then that my chest clenches, the ache terrible and fierce. Longing overwhelms me. For the deep sound of his voice rolling through me. For the way he made me feel. Not like I am now. A useless creature, deserving of contempt and ridicule.

7

'Well, let's see what we have available right now, shall we?' Jabel clicks at her keyboard and peers at her monitor, and I decide it's not in my imagination that she treats me with decidedly less warmth than before. Expected, I suppose, but still ironic considering that a little more than a month ago she invited me to every family gathering she hosted, plying me with food and drink and sitting me between Corbin and Cassian. Her son and her nephew. One way or another, she would have the fire-breather in her family. I've always known this was her goal.

I stand in front of her desk and try not to fidget. She's not looking at me right now, and for that I'm glad. I always avoid her gaze. Even though hypnos draki are unable to use their talent on fellow draki, I feel like she can get inside my head anyway, whispering her words, trying to influence my actions.

A deep rumble of voices flows from the office behind her. Severin, I'm sure. In there with the elders. At least I don't have to see him. Or worse—I don't have to endure some remark about losing my duty being the least of what I deserve.

'Ah, here we have something.'

I nod, eager to leave.

Grabbing a slip of paper, she starts scrawling, saying, 'There's always room on the gutting crew. I'm putting you down for Mondays, Wednesdays, and Fridays. Those are big hunting and fishing days. They can use an extra hand then.'

My stomach lurches. The gutting crew? I must have made a sound because Jabel gives me a sharp look. 'Too good to skin and gut the food that keeps us fed?'

I shake my head, but I'm sure the motion is slow, unconvincing. 'No, but . . . is there nothing else available?'

She snaps her gaze back to the paper and signs her name with a flourish. Ripping it from the pad, she hands it to me. 'Take this with you when you report in.'

I take the slip and exit the office, wondering whether I should have said anything at all about needing a new duty. Would anyone even notice if I went without one for a while?

Other than children who throw balls at my head, everyone else has been doing a good job ignoring me, treating me like I'm invisible. Even my own best friend avoids me.

As though the mere thought conjures her, I spot Az as I descend the steps. I call her name and hurry to catch up with her. She shoots a quick glance over her shoulder before whipping around again.

I'm panting by the time I reach her. 'Az, please, wait.'

'Why?' She keeps a brisk pace, staring straight ahead.

'C'mon, Az. I can handle lots of things, but not you being mad at me.'

'Really?' Her blue-black eyes flick to me. 'I wouldn't think that would matter.'

'Of course you matter to me.'

'Really?' She makes an ugly sound. 'I do? I didn't think anyone in this pride ranked over your human!' She stops now, fury sparking from her almond-shaped eyes. 'When you showed yourself to him did you think of me at all? About any of us?'

I search her face, pleading. 'Az, it wasn't like that. Will is—'

'Will,' she spits his name out, her hands knotted into fists at her sides. 'I never thought you would sell us out for some guy. The whole time you were gone I worried about you. Even when Severin imposed his stupid rules and curfews and everyone started grumbling it was because of you, I told them they were wrong. You never would have left deliberately. I was sure your mom made you. Kidnapped you or something. How stupid was I?' She shakes her head, her hair rippling like water around her. 'And the whole time you were probably off making out with some human . . . a hunter!'

'Az, please—'

'Were you ever going to tell me?'

'Eventually. Yes!'

She holds two hands up in the air like she wants to shove me from her. 'Sorry, Jacinda. I just can't talk to you right now.' She looks me up and down. 'I don't know you anymore.'

She spins, her blue-streaked hair a splash of color on the chalky air. I watch, helpless, spotting Miram in the road ahead. She waves Az over. I hold my breath, thinking surely Az has not taken to hanging out with her. But Az joins her and together they walk away.

I stand there for a moment, my throat impossibly thick. Then, conscious of how alone I am standing in the middle of the road, how pathetic I must look staring after my ex-best friend, I begin to move. One foot in front of the other. Left, right, left, right.

I should report in to my new duty. That would be the responsible thing to do. But I don't care. I've already failed everybody. I can't disappoint them any more than I have.

I toy with my dinner, moving food around my plate to make it look like I'm eating. Mom made verdaberry bread, but even that isn't enough to restore my appetite.

I glance out the kitchen window at the settling dusk, imagining Tamra and the others gathered in the field for group flight tonight. She stopped by earlier to see if I wanted to go. Selfish or not, I couldn't do it. I'm not ready to take to the sky with my sister and everyone else. In my dreams, when I had imagined things as they should be, it was always the two of us.

'How was your day?' Mom asks.

Something I would like to forget. Or at least make it until tomorrow so I can say it's officially behind me.

My gaze drifts to Tamra's vacant seat and I quickly look away . . . only to find myself staring at the space where Dad used to sit.

There's nowhere safe to look. I'm surrounded by emptiness. Dad's chair to my right. Tamra's across from me. It's only Mom to my left. And me.

'Fine.' I crumble a piece of bread between my fingers, squishing a verdaberry. Green juice stains my fingertips.

'Use your fork,' Mom says.

I pick up the utensil and stab at the dark bread. I'm not about to unload on her when she looks so fragile right now. If it hasn't been easy for me here, then I know it's been rough on her. Especially since the pride blames her for taking us away. 'And you?' I ask. 'What'd you do?'

She shrugs, twisting her thin shoulder as if to say nothing worth mentioning. I think of getting hit in the head with the ball and wonder if that happened to Mom, too. The thought makes me clench my fork so tightly my knuckles ache. 'It was good to see Tamra,' she volunteers.

'Yeah,' I second.

'She looks . . . good.'

'Yeah.' Pale as an icicle.

'Spending a lot of time with Cassian,' Mom adds, watching me closely to see how this affects me. 'She seems happy.'

I merely nod, unable to deny that. Tamra *did* look happy. But then she had Cassian now. Why wouldn't she be?

After a moment, Mom adds, 'I had a slow day at the clinic.'

'Well, that's always a good thing,' I murmur, glad Mom didn't lose her duty at the clinic. As a verda draki—or a *former* verda draki—her skills are best suited to working with the ill or injured, making the poultices and medicines that have kept our kind in good shape for generations. I don't see them reassigning her just out of spite. Doing so would be a disservice to the pride.

'Reorganized the meds,' she volunteers, her voice a numbing monotone. 'I don't think anyone's done that since I left.'

I nod slowly, gathering my nerve to confess: 'I was reassigned.' Hopefully my voice sounds as unaffected as hers. I have to tell her. She'd find out eventually. If not from me, then someone else.

I wait for the raised eyebrow, the sharp tone that will demand *why* they did that. Basically, I wait for the protective, vigilant mother she's always been.

Instead her voice sounds hollow. 'You're not in the library anymore?'

'No.' I take a bite and chew quickly, dreading the next words. 'I'm with the gutting crew.'

She looks up. 'The gutting crew?'

'Yeah.' I tear at the verdaberry bread until it's only crumbs. 'They needed some extra hands.'

'And who reassigned you to the gutting crew?' she asks quietly.

I give half a shrug, certain this is when she will lose her cool. 'Jabel gave me the assignment.'

Nothing.

Mom's quiet for a long moment, staring down at her plate before pushing up from the table and taking her dishes into the kitchen. I cringe as she drops them in the sink with a clatter. Still, I wait. Ready for her to say something, *do* something. March across the street and light into Jabel, her old friend. I can almost imagine the shouting, hear my mom demanding why her daughter was given such a lowly duty reserved for those training to be part of the pride's hunting crew.

That would be familiar. That would be typical.

Nothing. I strain for a sound and detect the uncorking of a bottle, the faint slosh of wine into a glass.

After a moment, she reemerges, stops at the table with a glass in hand, the deep green liquid dangerously close to the edge. She stares at me over the rim as she pulls a deep swallow of verda wine.

'Everything will be OK,' I say because I don't know *what* to say to her. She's not acting like Mom at all. 'I screwed up and they have to punish me. It will all blow over.'

She takes a slow sip, her eyes dull. 'Yeah. Guess you're right.' She disappears back into the kitchen again. When she returns it's with a full bottle of verda wine tucked between her arm and body. My gaze trails her as she walks down the hallway to her bedroom. The door clicks shut after her. A moment passes and I hear the low drone of the television from her room.

I sit at the table for a moment and glance around. At three empty chairs. I quickly stand, unable to sit there another moment.

Gathering the dishes, I take them to the sink. The silence in the kitchen is thick, Mom's television a distant hum. As I wash, my stare drifts up to the kitchen window and I bite back a gasp. A bowl slips from my hand, bounces off the edge of the sink, and shatters on the floor. Still, I don't move, don't even look to investigate the searing pain at the side of my foot.

My gaze fixes unblinking at the far side of Mom's withered-dead garden. A shape stands in the gloom. The eyes watching me seem to glow, to cut through the evening mist to my house. To me.

The mist swirls, drifts like smoke from a peat fire around him. It parts to reveal a face—Corbin's curling smile. He looks smug, pleased with himself as he stands there brazenly.

My skin snaps, lungs contract and swell, vibrating with warmth as my gaze narrows, reading perfectly into that smile.

He thinks I'm his for the taking. Tamra and Cassian have each other, and I'm out of favor with the pride—what else should I do but embrace the one draki who looks at me? Who wants me? Right? *Wrong*.

Smolder builds in my chest. He probably thinks I'll fall to my knees before him, grateful for whatever crumb he casts my way, salvation in this new friendless, lightless existence among my own kind.

Glaring at the shrouded figure, I snatch at the cord and the blinds fall into place with a noisy rattle. But still I imagine him there, see him staring back at me, watching, waiting.

It's strange. I'm back in the home I've longed for, in cool mists and air that weeps kisses over my thirsting flesh. But dead desert might as well surround me. Again. And this time there is no Will to revive me. There is nothing.

That night I make sure my window is locked. A precaution I never took before, even when I was in Chaparral, but for some reason I feel the need to do it tonight, with Corbin's glowing eyes imprinted on my mind.

8

Days pass quietly, like pages turning in a book, one after the other. As my life sinks into a routine, the loneliness bears deep, gnawing at me. Dusk settles as I walk home from work. The mist rides thick and the fading sunlight struggles to penetrate the opaque air, breaking through in patches here and there, staving off the night.

I hear him before I spot him. Cassian materializes in the mist before me, his tread soft on the path. We both stop and face each other. He lives on the other side of the township. I can guess the reason he's this far south. I know where he's coming from, where he's been. The same place he's been spending most of his time.

'Cassian,' I greet, twisting my fingers until they ache, rubbing at the flesh, as though the blood were still there from all the fish I cleaned today.

'Jacinda. How are you?' He asks this like we're polite acquaintances. And I guess we are in a way. We've become that. Since he decided to focus on my sister.

Suddenly I loathe the sight of him. I feel used, lied to. He never wanted me. Never really liked me for me.

The mist strokes my face as I glare up at Cassian, something inside me unraveling, like ribbons on a package coming undone.

Cassian stares down at me, his arms behind his back. Like Severin or another elder glowering down at me, and I guess he's on his way to being one of them.

My skin prickles with resentment. I hate it when he reminds me of them—of his father. It's a bitter pill after he almost convinced me he was different. I wanted to believe him. The words he told me in Chaparral when he was trying to get me to come home with him echo in my head.

There's something in you . . . you're the only thing real for me there, the only thing remotely interesting.

Lies to get me to trust him. Or he changed his mind. Either way, I don't interest him anymore. Not as Tamra does.

Finally, when I don't answer, he says, 'You've got to stop this.'

'Stop what?'

He dips his head, looks at me through shadowed eyes. 'Stop making it so damn hard on yourself. Pining for some—'

'I don't want to hear this.' I shake my head. 'Not that you really care, but I've let it go.' It's easier saying *it*. Even though we both know I mean Will.

'Then why do I still see him in your eyes?'

A hiss of pain escapes me.

I lash out with one knotted fist against his dense-muscled chest, taking out every frustration, every pain on him.

He doesn't move. I hit him again. Still nothing. He takes it. Stares at me from the impenetrable black of his eyes. With a strangled cry, I hit him again and again. Landing blows anywhere I can reach. My vision blurs, and I realize I'm crying.

This only infuriates me more. Breaking down in front of Cassian, losing control, succumbing to weakness as he stands witness . . .

'Jacinda,' he says, then again, louder, because I don't stop, can't stop the flurry of my fists on the solid wall of him. 'Enough!'

He stops me. I guess he always could have, but now he actually does it. He hauls me close, not so much a hug as a body lock, both arms wrapped around me.

It's disconcerting, our bodies so close, pressed tightly together. Our breaths fall in a fast, matching rhythm.

I pull back my head, look into his face. See him as I never have.

He's no longer looking *at* me. It feels like he's looking inside me, his gaze probing. Accepting me for me. A closeness I haven't felt with anyone since I arrived here sweeps through me. And it's a promise of an end to my numbing loneliness. If I let it happen. Let *this* happen.

I panic again. Because it's Cassian.

A sob strangles in my throat and spills raggedly from my lips. I close my eyes in a long and miserable blink and pull myself together again. Wrenching from his warm embrace, I barrel past him.

He grabs my arm as I pass and swings me around like we're doing a dance move.

I glare at that hand on my arm. 'Let me go.'

He's quiet for a moment, his chest rising and falling

with breath. 'What's this really about? Why are you running from me?'

I say nothing at first, the only noise the crashing of my ragged breath. Then, I burst. 'You lied to me!'

He cuts the murky air with one of his big, crushing hands. 'When have I lied to you?'

I continue as if I don't hear him. And I don't. Not really. It's finally gotten to me—how quickly he dropped me once Tamra manifested. 'I wasn't special to you. You just saw the fire-breather. Like everyone else. It was never me.' And now it's Tamra. Only it's not her either. She's only one thing to him, and everyone else—the pride's precious shader.

Now I know. Now I see him for what he is.

'I've only ever been honest with you.' His nostrils flare, ridges popping up on the bridge of his nose, rising in and out with the surge of his temper. I should back down at the sight, but then I've never been one to do what I should.

'Right,' I spit out.

He's shaking now, his eyes more purple than black. 'You want to hear some truth, Jacinda? How about this? I can't stand the sight of you. Not when you're moping around here like someone who needs to be on a suicide watch . . . all for a guy who's probably already forgotten about you and moved on to the next hunt.'

My fingers curl into fists, cutting into my palms. I want to say so much right then—mostly that Will hasn't forgotten me. But I shouldn't argue this point. I should hope it's true. I've vowed to let Will go, but a desperate hunger for him still twists through me—a viper writhing through my body, working its poison.

73

I don't have Will. I have nothing. Nothing but a frantic need to grab on to something, anything to keep me afloat in the desert of my existence.

Instead, I say, 'And me dead would just break you up, wouldn't it?'

He stares at me so starkly, incredulous. 'You think I'd want you dead?' His eyes are wide and searching. They make me start to doubt myself, that maybe he does care about me. I begin to shake as confusing thoughts and feelings whirl through me. 'What do you want from me, Jacinda?'

I glance at his hand still on my arm. My skin swims with heat, especially where he touches me.

'Let me go.' He stands so close, towering over me, making me feel small when I'm not. 'I have to go,' I say louder. And I do. I have to go. Now.

In answer, his skin blurs, his darker draki flesh flashing in and out beneath his human skin, reminding me of what he is. What I am. And I can't help remembering how everyone always thought we were perfectly matched. Now they think that about him and Tamra.

His lip curls back from his teeth, the white startling against his olive-hued skin. 'Why? So you can be alone? Is that what you prefer? Gutting fish in the day and then crying into your pillow at night? That's what you want? Has it occurred to you that I haven't pulled away from you as much as you've pushed me away? You're nothing but a selfish, scared little girl who'd rather lick her wounds than live.'

His words strike deep, arrowing directly for the heart. Too close to the truth. *You're nothing but a selfish, scared little girl . . .*

My vision shifts, grows crisper, and I know I'm staring out at him through vertical pupils. Steam eats up my throat, burns through my mouth and nostrils.

I stagger back a step. He doesn't move this time. He lets me go.

Turning, I sprint through damp air until my lungs burn and feel ready to burst from my too-tight chest. I revel in it—a pleasure that borders on pain, a welcome distraction. Even as I slow my pace, I vow to keep going, keep walking until I've regained composure. Until I no longer feel Cassian's arms around me. Until I no longer hear his words. *Selfish, scared little girl. Selfish, scared little girl.*

Damn him for getting in my head. For maybe being right.

The red-gold beams of fading dusk filter down through the mist. The fiery light touches my skin in flashes, gilding me here and there, reminding me of how I look in full manifest—of what I am. What I will always be. The desert hadn't killed it. Nothing can.

I feel certain of that now. My draki will never fade. Maybe it's all I know anymore.

I survived my mother's attempt to kill off my draki. I survived the desert, hunters all around me with their hungry gazes, the fear so thick I could taste it in my mouth. After all that, I know my draki is here to stay. I don't have to worry about losing that part of myself anymore. I should be happy. Relieved.

Except I'm not. My eyes sting and I blink them rapidly.

Inhaling deeply, I move. My chest rises, fills with the aroma of sweet, arable earth. I'm sustained here. Even if my soul yearns for more. For Will.

Anger surges through me. I'm crazy to yearn for a boy lost to me forever. Why can't I move on and find what happiness I can with the pride?

Then I see it sketched against the hazy twilight. The dilapidated tower stretches up through the fog like an ancient, twisting tree covered in thick, wiry vines. It's not as tall as the other three watchtowers strategically positioned throughout the township, but it's the oldest, the first, built back when the idea of existing without a shader seemed impossible, a reality for which we needn't prepare.

Time changed that attitude. As Nidia aged and no other shader manifested, fear set in that the next generation of draki would be without a shader. The other towers were built then, stronger—taller than before—in preparation for the days to come when we would have to rely on ourselves to safeguard the township.

I stop at the base and look up. Watchtowers are always camouflaged with vines and bramble, the better to blend them with the natural landscape, but this one looks more natural than the others. And I love that. Love the wildness of it as it returns to nature. It hasn't been used in years, since before I was born, but I remember this forgotten tower well, my childhood haunt.

I lay my hand on a weathered rung and begin to climb. An animal, startled by my intrusion, scurries up the twisted beams as I ascend.

I push through the congestion of leaves. Wiry branches poke me, grab my hair like sharp fingers as I climb higher and higher. Rotting wood creaks beneath me. I reach the top and drop onto my back on the moss-speckled wood with a sigh.

I splay a hand over my stomach, feel myself breathe in and out, my lungs expanding. And it all comes back to me. My love for this place. A place I can safely exist. Where I can be me. Away from prying eyes.

A canopy of green covers me. I spot the sky drifting overhead through gaps in the wood and foliage. Sitting up, I cross my legs and stare out at the vast, pulsing green world spread below. The pride is there. The green-tiled roofs peep out through Nidia's mist.

Mist curls between the houses and buildings, covering the fields, crawling over the township's walls and spreading across the land like a living thing, settling thickly into the valleys and over the lesser hills and mountains in a foamy white. Only the tallest treetops poke through the mantle of fog.

'Thought I'd find you here.'

I shrink into myself, pulling my knees close to my chest as Cassian's dark head emerges, followed by the rest of him. He lowers down beside me, the wood groaning in protest.

'This is probably a deathtrap, you know. It should have been torn down a long time ago.'

'It would be sacrilege. There are too many memories attached to it,' I say. 'No one can do it.'

He reaches down and strokes a moss-lined board. 'Yeah. That's the truth. Wonder how many first kisses were stolen up here.'

Something tightens a little inside me at this. My first kiss wasn't here. It was with Will. Out there. My gaze drifts to the vast world spread out below me, so different from the desert where my heart found Will. It probably should have been here. It probably *would* have been here if I hadn't left.

77

I inhale cool, damp air through my nostrils. 'Why did you follow me?'

Cassian's voice rumbles on air as dense as the drape of night closing around us, sealing us in. 'Did you think I wouldn't?'

I say nothing. He stares at me with his impenetrable gaze. Rain starts to fall in earnest then, the patter amplifying the stretch of silence between us. The water finds its way through the holes and cracks in the canopy above us and drops coldly upon my hair. I don't mind. I've never minded the cold.

Cassian angles his head, water sitting on the sleek, dark strands like beads of crystal. 'You really think I wouldn't care if you were dead?'

I pull back, remembering that I had accused him of not caring what happened to me.

'I've been avoiding you because I'm just so damn annoyed . . .' He shakes his head, sloshing water. The strands brush his shoulders rhythmically. 'I don't want you risking yourself again. The human world . . . Will. It's too dangerous.' Cassian takes my hand. I feel his heartbeat through the simple touch, the thud of his life meeting with mine. 'You dead . . . it would break me.' His voice whips sharply over the drum of rainfall. 'Everything I ever said to you was the truth. My feelings haven't changed for you, Jacinda. Even if you do drive me crazy, here, in the pride . . . you're still that single bright light for me.'

I don't know who moved first.

Maybe it was both of us. Or maybe I just don't want to accept that it might have been me. Might have been *my* head inching forward, my wet face lifting up to his. My heart beating so loud it thundered like a drum in my chest.

His lips are soft at the first brush. One of us trembles. Me or him. Both of us? I don't know, don't care.

It's a feathery kiss, lips brushing, grazing, tasting, almost as if we are afraid of startling each other. And we are.

Even as exhilarated as I feel in this moment, I'm not totally unaware of what's happening—of the strangeness of me kissing Cassian. It's terrifying to do this thing that has been unthinkable for so long. But I guess buried underneath it all, tension has always been a humming wire stretched tightly between us. Tonight I let go of my end and the wire snaps free. Before Will, I had wondered about Cassian and me, wondered about us—together. I had thought *maybe*. Even if I never admitted it to myself, never could because of Tamra. Because I was *told* that we would be together someday and not *asked*.

Yet, even knowing all this, I don't stop. Don't pull away and run.

The gentle play of his rain-wet lips on mine is sweet, exciting. I lean into him, taste mint on his mouth. My heart warms, softens to have this intimacy, this connection to another soul again.

Until the kiss changes.

The pressure increases ever so slightly. The intensity deepens into something that I feel in my bones, in the sudden snap of my flesh and hot rush of my blood. His lips grow more demanding, hard and soft at the same time, devouring my mouth.

I moan and he quickly pulls back, brushing my face with his fingers. 'Is this OK—'

Nodding, I pull him back to me, needing this too much right now. I can't feel anything but an easing of the ache that's been gnawing away inside me since leaving Chaparral.

He embraces his hunger.

Strange animal sounds come from him. Or is that me?

Vibrations rumble from my chest, climb up my contracting windpipe. I wedge my arms between us and turn my palms into his chest, craving touch, the sensation of another. I unfurl my fingers so my palms lie flat on his chest. His heart thuds steady and strong.

His hand drags up my back, buries in my wet hair, catching in the thick snarls, but I don't care. I revel in it, in the knowledge of another's desire for me—for Cassian's desire.

His palm cups the back of my skull, cradling my head.

His lips slide from my mouth to my slippery jaw. His teeth nip there and I can't stop myself. I sigh, feel the pull in my flesh, the snap of my skin and know that I'm no longer entirely human. He's brought the draki to life in me. *Just like Will did.*

The thought makes me jerk, suck in a watery breath. I break away, gasping icy air into my smoldering lungs, stare into his eyes, the deepest purple, the pupils thin, dark vertical slits.

Horrified, I brush a hand over my burning mouth before dragging fingers against my skin, feeling its tight, smooth texture and confirming that I've halfway manifested. Because of him.

His own skin flashes in and out, dark glittering charcoal. 'Jacinda.' I drop my gaze to his mouth, to the lips I tasted with my own. They're a deep shade of pink, swollen and bruised-looking from kissing. Nausea swells inside me. No, no, no, no . . .

I shake my head savagely and mutter to myself. *Wrong.* What am I doing? How could I do this to Tamra?

The answer comes to me. I kissed him, *seized* him, because I could. Because I'm lonely. Because he's here, wanting me, accepting me. He's here. And Will's not.

That's all there is to it. He's not what I really want. Not *who* I want.

'Jacinda,' he whispers.

'I have to go,' I say quickly, shoving wet hair back from my face. 'Mom will wonder where I am.' This isn't true, but I say it anyway.

'Jacinda,' he tries again.

'No,' I say, my voice sharp. 'This isn't going to happen, Cassian. This isn't fair to—' I stop myself.

'To Tamra,' he supplies.

'And you,' I return. 'You deserve someone who can give you everything. Tamra can do that.'

'You can, too,' he returns with such conviction that a small shiver runs through me. 'C'mon. You're getting cold,' he replies, misreading my shiver for a chill. Taking my hand, he guides me to the ladder and lets me descend first.

On the ground, he squints through rain up into the sky. 'No flying tonight.'

'Yeah.'

'Tamra's looking forward to flying with you. She's disappointed you haven't come out with her yet.'

'I know.'

'Next time? Will you come?'

'Yeah,' I say, meaning it.

Nothing has changed. I have to adjust back into pride life. I have to forget Will. I have to forget about kissing Cassian. I'll forget and adjust, and everything will be all right.

We walk through the rain to my house. Cassian follows me up to my door. 'See you tomorrow.' His voice is husky as he stares down at me, his eyes different, softer almost. My stomach knots as he turns away.

'Cassian.' I skip down the steps and back into the rain, determined that he understand we're only friends. We can never be more than that.

Holding a hand over my eyes, I look up at him. 'Thanks. I'm glad we're . . . friends.' I say the word *friends* deliberately, letting the emphasis get my point across.

His mouth curves with a slow smile. 'I've never wanted to be your friend, Jacinda.'

My heart stutters in my chest. Standing in the pouring rain, I watch him walk away.

9

The rain finally stops after three days. Alone on my front porch, I look up from my lunch as the rippling veil of gray dies a sudden death. Almost instantly, Nidia's fog rolls in, like something living, pulsing with breath. It quickly cloaks the township. The umbrella I used when walking home from school swivels on its side on the porch from the sudden shift in air.

I'd just returned from Evasive Maneuvers, and flight patterns dance in my head like constellations as I nibble on a slice of verdaberry bread. I have to head back for my afternoon class shortly, but for now I enjoy the quiet. Kicking off my shoes, I let the mist slide over my bare feet.

Mom's at work. They keep scheduling her long hours, giving her back-to-back shifts. Deliberately, of course. I've seen so little of her. Living with Nidia, Tamra sees her even less. They want it that way.

Without the drumming of rain, the abrupt silence feels eerie, like the world is holding its breath around me. I set my plate down and pull the throw from the back of the bench. The dry heat of Chaparral is a distant memory as I burrow into the fleece.

Across the street, the hazy figure of Corbin steps from his house. As my gaze lands on his blue armband, something clenches in my stomach.

His eyes immediately find me. With a wave, he saunters across the street and stops at the bottom step of my porch. Holding a hand up as if grasping the air, he smiles. 'Guess we're flying tonight.'

I force a smile. He's my neighbor. He's not going anywhere. And neither am I. Despite how distasteful I find him, I have to tolerate him. 'Yeah. Rain finally quit.'

'You joining us then?'

I nod. I promised I would . . . and I want to. I need to fly again. Especially with the sister I never thought I would get the chance to fly *with*. We'll be able to share the sky at last. 'Yes.'

'Good.' Hues of purply black glint in his fair hair as he nods. 'It's good to see you coming around, Jacinda.'

This I can't let pass. 'I'm not coming around for you.'

His lips twitch. 'But you're coming around.'

He looks down the street then, staring for a long moment as if he sees something coming our way through the cool vapor. 'I saw your sister this morning.'

I reveal nothing as I look at him, even as wariness trickles through me. He voiced his intentions. He wants one of us—is determined to have one of us.

'She and Cassian were going to the orchards with some others. She looked . . . happy.'

'She is,' I say.

And why shouldn't she be? She has what she's always wanted. Friendship, acceptance by her own kind . . . *Cassian*. If I don't mess that up for her. The nasty guilt that's been eating at me for the last three days, ever since that kiss with Cassian, takes another bite at my conscience.

'I'll come by after my shift ends and we can walk together to the flight field.'

I bristle. This is the Corbin I remember. The arrogant boy who never asks but simply takes. 'I already have plans to meet up with Tamra.'

His mouth twists. 'You can't hide behind your sister forever.' He turns and starts down the path. 'See you tonight,' he calls over his shoulder.

I watch his figure fading into the quivering mist and wonder what it will take to make him forget about me.

'You're avoiding me.'

I look up as I descend the school's front steps. Cassian pushes off from a column and falls in beside me. He's correct, of course. I have been avoiding him. But I don't admit this.

'It's been raining nonstop,' I say instead.

'I like the rain,' he responds thickly, and I know he's thinking about our kiss in the rain. Something I've had a hard time putting out of my head.

I slide him a look, study the sleek fall of his hair. My breath quickens. Hugging my book to my chest, I stride ahead.

Cassian keeps up. 'Why are you avoiding me?'

'I'm not avoiding you,' I lie. 'I just haven't gone out of my way looking for you. Did you expect I would . . .' *after that kiss* . . . Guilty heat floods my face. I shoot him a glance. 'Aren't you a little old to be hanging out around the school? You finished up last term.'

'How else am I going to catch you?'

'Um, I don't know. At my house maybe.'

I can't help wondering whether he doesn't want to risk Tamra hearing about him coming to visit me at home. The two of us seen together like this . . . out and about town—not such a big deal. This can be chalked up to coincidence. If that's the case, he's not so immune to Tamra after all. I frown a little, wondering why this prospect doesn't fill me with immediate relief. Isn't that what I want? For him to like my sister as much as she likes him? I walk faster.

'We need to talk.' He grabs me by the arm and forces me to face him.

'About what, Cassian?'

'The other day—'

Panic claws up my throat. 'Was a mistake,' I finish, determined that he sees it that way, too.

Something passes over his face. An emotion I've never seen in him. Come to think of it, emotion from him is pretty rare—period.

'Cassian! Wait up!'

We both turn. Miram is behind us, hurrying to catch up.

I mutter something unkind. Others might be softening toward me, but not Miram. She continues to look at me as though I've done something to her.

I start to go, but Cassian holds my arm. I stare down at his fingers, then look back at his face. 'She didn't call *my* name. Do me a favor and let me go.'

Cassian frowns and his dark eyes drill into me. 'This isn't over,' he murmurs.

'Yeah.' I nod, cool resolve stealing over me. 'It is.' Twisting my arm free, I march away before Miram reaches us.

* * *

We gather in the flight field at the far north of the township. Close to thirty of us have arrived in our usual robes, garments easy to discard and don again.

Tall pines shroud the clearing. Beyond the field, mountains spill in a jagged line several shades darker than the murky night.

Even Severin joins us, although not robed, so presumably he's only keeping an eye on us and not flying out tonight. He catches sight of me, and I don't miss the flash of approval crossing his face. Despite not wanting to care, something lightens in my chest. This is what I've decided to do after all. Put everything behind me. Set aside my selfish desires that only bring hurt to others. Move on with my life here and forget the feelings I have for a boy who isn't meant for me.

So that means getting along with everyone. Even Severin.

Holding his clipboard, our flight master looks us over, taking count.

Traditionally, we're assigned a flight partner. Someone we can't separate from at any time. Immediately, I step up next to Tamra, stake my claim. Tonight, we'll fly together.

I spot Az and feel a pinch in my heart when I notice she's paired with Miram. She sees me, too, holds my stare. For a moment, I think she is going to come over, but then she looks away.

'She'll come around,' Tamra says. 'She's afraid.'

'Afraid? Of what?'

'That she's lost you.'

'But she's the one avoiding me!'

'Yeah, but she's in control of that. She can't control you or anything else that's happened. Not having any control over what matters in your life . . . well, that scares people.'

I shake my head with a smile. 'When did you get so smart?'

She winks at me. 'Hate to break it to you, but I've always been the smarter twin.'

I snort and give her a light punch on the shoulder even as an easy warmth sweeps through me. I still have Tamra. Maybe more than I ever did before. Maybe we'll be like we used to be when we were little girls, before I manifested. We have common ground again. Standing beside Tamra, I think of Dad. How happy he would be if he could see us standing here now.

Feeling a swell of emotion, I look away. And that's when I see Cassian. Instantly my lips tingle with memory.

He's watching me with his intense purply dark gaze. I feel a surge of guilt. Here I am, standing beside my sister, reveling in our newfound closeness with the secret of my kiss with Cassian hovering unspoken between us.

'Hey, there's Cassian!' Tamra waves him over cheerfully.

As Cassian heads our way, Corbin falls into step beside him. A look passes between the two cousins as they approach us. It's not friendly, but then the two have never pretended to like each other. Corbin has never disguised the fact that he wants to be the pride's next alpha, that he believes himself a better candidate. In that way, he reminds me a lot of Xander, Will's cousin.

'So you both made it.' Cassian smiles and I know he understands just how special, how momentous this is for Tamra and me.

I say hello back, keeping my voice small, like it might make me less noticeable . . . make our kiss something forgettable, something that didn't happen.

'Thought it would never stop raining,' Corbin says, rubbing his hands together in anticipation. 'I need to hit some wind.'

Tamra nods, looking like an eager child. 'Yeah, me too,' she says as though she's been doing this for years. I fight back my smile.

'Got a partner, yet, Cassian?' Corbin asks.

Cassian hesitates. 'No.'

'Cool. You and me then.'

I frown, wondering when was the last time these two paired up during group flight. They're so competitive . . .

I don't ponder it for long because our flight master calls us to the center of the darkened field. Perimeter lights line the edge, there for when we land and when we play a night game of airball. Not that it's necessary. Most of us have excellent night vision. I shoot Tamra a glance. *Most* of us. This is still new to her.

We stand in our pairs. When the signals are given, we will each drop our robes, manifest, and take off two at a time. Tamra and I wait behind Cassian and Corbin, but I don't even look at them.

Shoulder to shoulder with my sister, I absorb the significance of this moment. Our first flight together. Dad always expected we would have this. It broke his heart when we never did.

We would listen raptly in our beds as he talked to us about flying, Mom smiling on indulgently, never getting it, never understanding his love for the sky and wind. As much as Dad loved her, he wanted us to be like him. At least in the way he loved to fly. And tonight we would.

Before we drop our robes, Tamra's hand reaches out and squeezes mine. She looks so happy, so at peace with herself, that I know this is right. Me, here with the pride—it's where I should be. In this moment, I can believe everything will be OK.

Leaving our robes behind, we shed our human layers, too.

The familiar pull begins in my chest as my human exterior melts away, fades, replaced with my thicker draki skin.

I tilt my face up to the night, feel my cheeks tightening, bones stretching and sharpening. My breathing changes, deepens, as my nose shifts, cartilage crackling as the ridges appear along the bridge. My limbs loosen, extend longer. This drag of my bones feels good, like a nice long stretch after being stuck in a car for endless hours.

My wings push out from behind me, and I sigh, reveling in their release. They unfurl with a whisper, slightly longer than the length of my back. I work them, let the wiry sheets of fiery gold test the air.

Far up in the sky, I note the sifting clouds, like smoke on the dark night. I can't wait to cut through them, feel the vapor on my skin. I look down at my body; my skin glows like light through amber. My gaze drifts to my sister and my breath catches at the sight of her. She's beautiful with her iridescent, silvery white skin—the moon to my sun.

'Ready?' I ask in our rumbling draki-speech, the only language I can speak in full manifest due to the changes in my vocal cords. But this is the first time Tamra can answer in the ancient language of our forefathers, true dragons.

Her eyes—enlarged irises and dark vertical pupils—stare back at me. 'Yes,' she rumbles, and I know she's been yearning for this all her life.

She launches smoothly from the earth. I push off with the balls of my feet into the damp air, letting Tamra creep higher so that I can watch, in awe at the sight of her: the silvery pearl of her draki skin; the gossamer wings that twinkle like sheets of glinting ice.

She glows like a white star against the dark night. Looking back, she calls, 'C'mon, I thought you were fast. Show me!'

I smile wide, and wind rushes over me as I catch up to her in a soaring twirl. It seems forever since I've had this. Even without the taste of sun on my flesh, it's a wonderful sensation to fly again.

Tamra moves cautiously, distrustful of her own ability, of the air currents roaring past us. We fall to the back of the group.

Others whip past us, their shouts lost on the roaring winds as they twirl in flashes of color: Az's iridescent blue with its winks of pink; the glimmering bronze of my fellow earth draki. I spot Miram, her flesh a dull tan. The onyx among us are the hardest to detect, their iridescent black and purple flesh blends well into the night. Another reason why, historically, they're our best fighters. No one sees them coming.

I slow down, identifying Corbin and Cassian, flying at incredible speeds through the night, wind whistling to a shrill pitch around them as they race in wild zigzags to some unknown finish line. They weave and dart around each other, just short of collision. I shake my head. Still the same idiot boys showing off for the pride . . . or, in this case, Tamra. Or *you*, a voice whispers in my head, but I quickly shove it back with a vicious swipe.

Tamra shouts again, 'Jacinda! C'mon!'

I pull back my wings and surge forward, tempering my speed when I hear my sister's wings slapping fiercely to keep up.

Side by side, we soar together. This is enough, I think. More than I ever dreamed. As everyone else leaves us behind, we don't care. We laugh and spin in the wind, break through the vaporous night, moving and manipulating the air like a pair of children exploring the water of a swimming pool.

A childhood joy we've never felt. Before now.

10

'Why don't you come back to the house? We can roast some root seeds and watch movies,' I suggest as Tamra and I walk back from the field. My body still tingles, awake and alive from our recent flight in a way that I haven't felt since . . . I frown, forbidding the memory to intrude and ruin my new sense of peace.

'Sure,' she says.

I smile, thinking about all the late nights when Mom, Tamra, and I would squeeze onto the couch and watch movies—and then I remember how little I've seen Mom lately. She's probably asleep, wiped out from her long shift. When I left her after dinner she mentioned she might go to bed after her shower.

'Maybe Mom can join us.'

'Yeah,' I hedge, 'if she's still awake.'

Tamra sends me a look. I know what she's thinking: Mom always used to wait up for us if we were out doing anything. But that was before. Back when she felt she had some control over our world.

I open my mouth to explain the situation with Mom but stop . . . close my mouth and listen, peering into the waves of milky fog rolling around us, thicker than usual.

'Jacinda?'

'Something's wrong,' I say quietly, holding up a hand.

Even though no alarm sounds on the air, something is off. The township is an eerie quiet. It's still half an hour until curfew but no one is out walking except those of us returning from the flight field. They were having a jako tournament tonight at the rec center, but as we pass the center of town, the building is dark. The clink of gems used in the game can't be heard. Nor can the usual shouts of defeat or victory when someone's gem knocks another player's gem off the board.

Then, through the mist, one of the elders appears. It's almost comical to see his dignified figure running. 'Tamra. You're needed. Go at once to Nidia's. Hurry.'

It doesn't cross my mind to stay behind. We race through town, leaving the elder behind. Our steps thunder on the path. A small crowd stands gathered before Nidia's house. Severin and another elder, two guards with their blue armbands, Nidia and Jabel.

It's the combination of Nidia and Jabel that alerts me to the situation, jerks me to a halt. Someone has trespassed into the pride.

Tamra continues a few feet and then stops when she notices I'm not with her anymore. She looks back at me and then to the group, clearly uncertain. I can't speak. Can say nothing. My body won't move.

Nidia and Jabel only ever come together for one reason—when a trespasser enters the pride. Nidia may be more valued for her ability to shade the mind, but Jabel is useful, too. As a hypnos draki, she mesmerizes, planting lies in a human's head to fill the vacant gaps Nidia leaves.

The beating of my heart takes on a desperate rhythm. Heat flares, a wild, fiery burn in the back of my throat.

I strain for a good glimpse of the trespasser. Most of his figure is blocked by the others and a thick fog of mist. I identify his back, the outline of broad shoulders. I swallow against the scald in my throat and take a step closer, my hands balled into fists so tightly that a nail breaks and splinters against the tender flesh of one palm.

Footsteps rush behind me and I look over my shoulder. Several others have followed us. Cassian, Corbin, Miram, and Az . . .

'Tamra!' Severin sees her then. He shouts at her like she's an animal to be commanded, waves sharply with one hand. 'Come!'

Tamra moves ahead into the group and blocks what little view I have. Frowning, I draw closer, my steps slow, stilling to a stop when Tamra whirls around. Her gaze collides with mine.

The blood surges in my veins.

Her face says it all.

No. No, no, no . . .

It can't be him.

I start to shake my head, wanting to deny it, but most of all wanting Tamra to turn around and act natural so Severin and the others don't become suspicious.

And then the crowd shifts and I see Will. My gaze devours him, eyes staring so hard they ache. The stubborn honey brown hair still falls over his brow. The hard-set jaw looks as implacable as ever. He's here. Will kept his promise to me. And then I think, no. Will can't have remembered that promise. It's impossible. Tamra shaded him. Maybe he's here accidentally. Maybe he got lost from his group and stumbled into our midst . . .

My lips move, but say nothing. I dare not. Shaking my head, I wonder if I've imagined him, conjured him where he's not likely to be.

For a moment, joy swells inside me, before the terror of seeing him here, in the township, mere feet from Severin, slams into me.

He turns to answer something Nidia asks him— probably the details of how exactly he got lost, alone, this far up on the mountain, away from any major road. I stare hard at him, make out the carved lines of his features in the deep shadow of evening, in the perpetual swirl of fog.

Then he sees me, and I know it's not just simple recognition there. His hazel eyes gleam with such deep satisfaction that I know he remembers. Somehow. Someway. He remembers everything. He remembered his promise to me, and he's keeping it.

He's here for me.

Thankfully, my sister stops gawking at me before anyone notices and starts to wonder at her behavior. I give my head a swift shake, warning Will to take caution, to show no recognition. He shifts his head, the most imperceptible of nods, and I know he understands.

Every fiber of my being burns and pulses to cross the distance separating us. My hands open and close at my sides, yearning to touch, to feel him. To *feel* that it's really him. Here. Now. For his voice to ripple through me as it used to do. That stroke of velvet revived me in Chaparral, got me through my time there, filling the stretch of my days then, and filling my dreams since.

Everything else slips away as I stare at him. Where we are. The danger that still threatens . . .

Deep down, I know Tamra won't reveal Will's identity, and not just because of her loyalty to me. My sister's not a killer, and she knows one word from her would end his life. Right or wrong, she wouldn't do that. It's not in her.

But that hardly means he's safe.

The air stirs as someone steps up next to me and I turn to see Cassian staring across the distance at Will. For a moment, I had actually forgotten there was someone else who could recognize Will. I follow his gaze, the air hard to breathe, too thick to drag inside my constricting lungs as I process that Cassian is staring at Will—*here on his turf.* The boy he nearly killed when they rolled off a cliff. Sick misery coils like a serpent in the pit of my stomach.

Nothing's stopping Cassian from finishing that fight. He's not like Tamra. It's in him, down to his very essence, to kill. Onyx draki have been killing for thousands of years. That's what they do best. Right now, in this moment, I'm caught in a living nightmare.

I look back at Will. Two armed sentries that I went to primary school with flank him like he's a prisoner. If he's lucky, they won't see him for what he is . . . what he means to me. Nidia will simply shade him—useless as that seems to be—and send him on his way. As long as I stay calm. As long as Will gives nothing away. As long as Cassian doesn't say or *do* anything.

I sneak a fearful glance at Cassian, silently willing him to say nothing—to hold silent and spare Will's life.

His expression is tight, almost pained as he stares intently at me. 'Please,' I mouth, all I dare risk as Miram steps up, her arms folded across her chest in a militant pose.

'Hiker?' she asks.

Still staring at me, Cassian answers, 'Looks like it.'

'They gonna try Tamra out on him?' Corbin wonders aloud.

'Probably,' Miram says, stretching on her tiptoes in an attempt to peer into the group to see the *hiker*.

I resist moving closer, not about to look too curious and alert them that Will and I aren't strangers.

'He's young,' Miram muses. 'Cute, too.'

Az snorts. 'For a human, I guess.'

'For a human,' Miram agrees, sending me a sly glance. 'What do you think, Jacinda? You're the expert on cute humans. How does he compare?'

Heat tingles in my face, and I fight to look blasé, calm in the face of her jibes.

'That's enough, Miram,' Cassian snaps.

'Look,' Corbin quickly says, 'they're taking him into the house.' He laughs low. 'That guy won't know what hit him.'

Will doesn't look in my direction as he's led inside the cottage, but I know he's as aware of me as I am of him. My entire body hums in response to him. What was he thinking? He had to know how dangerous it would be to come anywhere near the pride. The truth is painful to face. *As much as I tried to forget him, he never forgot me.* Did that make him stronger than me? Or weaker?

Everyone goes inside except the two guards. They remain just outside the door. If all goes smoothly, Nidia will do what she does best, assisted by Jabel. Tamra, too, I suppose. Then the panicked thought hits me that Jabel's talent *will* work on him. What if she succeeds and he comes out of there confused and bewildered, with a head full of lies, unable to discern reality from fiction?

I twist my fingers until they ache. There's nothing I can do except wait. And hope he remembers again.

And what then? He knows where the pride is . . . where I am. He's seen me. He'll come back. If he's caught again they'll know he's different—that shading won't work on him.

'C'mon.' Cassian takes my arm. 'I'll walk you home.'

I resist only a moment. Of course I should go. The last thing I should do is linger here and give anyone cause to suspect that the trespasser means something to me.

Turning, I let Cassian lead me away. One thought pounds through my head in beat with my thundering heart: He kept his promise. He came for me.

Unable to help myself, I start to look over my shoulder, but Cassian's voice stops me. 'Don't look back, Jacinda.'

I force my gaze forward. He's right. The fact that Will remembers and came for me changes nothing. I can't go with him. I won't let my heart overrule logic. Nothing has changed. We're a dangerous combination. Like fire and oil.

Cassian says nothing else until we reach my house. 'Where's your mother?' he asks.

I motion for him to wait as I go check on Mom. She's asleep with the television on in her room, her features relaxed in a way I never see anymore. I quietly ease past the bed and turn off the TV. Closing her door, I return to where Cassian paces the living room.

His liquid-dark gaze cuts to me. 'How did he find—'

'I'm sure it was simple luck. He got too close to the township and patrol picked him up,' I quickly insert, not wanting him to realize that Will might be resistant to shading.

He shoots me an exasperated look. 'Jacinda, he's no innocent hiker.'

'Yeah. I know.' I fold my arms across my chest. 'He's a hunter.' A heavy silence stretches as I stare at him. 'So why didn't you say anything?'

'How do you know I won't?'

'Will you?'

He sets his jaw at a stubborn angle, like he wants to say yes, but then he blows out a deep breath and briefly looks away, and I can't tell whether he's angrier with me or himself.

'So you can hate me? So I can watch them kill him? I would get no satisfaction in that.'

I can only stare, no longer so surprised that Cassian might truly care for *me*. Me and not simply what I am. He's not my enemy. I believe he wants to help me. Why else would he bother protecting a boy I shouldn't even care about?

'You have to let him go, Jacinda.'

I nod, but the motion is painful, makes my temples throb. 'I know.'

'But *he* needs to know that,' he says, his voice heavy with meaning.

I meet his gaze, understanding dawning slowly. 'You want me to speak with him?'

'Once he's a good distance from the pride, you need to confront him and explain to him that it's over between the two of you. I know he might be confused after being shaded, but you need to get through to him.'

I can't look at him just then, not with what I suspect—that Will *can't* be shaded. Would Cassian be as willing to let him go if he thought that?

100

Cassian steps closer and turns my chin to look at him. 'Tell him to convince his family that this area is dry. That there aren't any draki here anymore. We've moved on. They'll listen to him.' The implication hangs there unsaid. *They'll listen to him because of the blood. Because he's connected to us.* Cassian lowers his face so close I can feel his breath on my cheek, and the memory of our kiss intrudes. If that isn't enough to make me recoil, then his next words are. 'If I see him here again, I won't hide the truth anymore—whether you hate me for it or not. I won't protect him again. Understand?'

I nod, a lump clogging my throat.

'C'mon.' He opens the front door to the misty night.

'Where are we going?' I ask.

'They'll probably drop him in the usual spot. I want you waiting for him when he comes out.'

11

I sip silent breaths from where I hide in a tree, the bark a rough scratch on my bare legs, needles poking me on all sides as I stare down at the spot where intruders who've been shaded are always dropped. It's not far from the public road that carves deep into the mountain, the only official road this high. My heart still thunders in my ears from my mad dash to get here first.

The patrol moves quietly through the woods, but even so, I hear their slight rustling as they approach. Ludo breaks through the trees with Will slung over his shoulder, Remy right behind him. Wincing, I watch as Ludo drops Will unceremoniously to the hard ground. That had to hurt. If Will is faking unconsciousness and is actually awake, as I suspect, he did a good job masking any reaction to such rough treatment.

The two draki stare down at him for a moment. Remy nudges him sharply with his boot.

'C'mon,' Ludo says. 'I'm hungry.'

I wait several moments after they leave, scanning the

trees, making certain nothing moves and they are well and truly gone. Will lies on the ground very still, dead still, and I can't wait any longer.

I climb down and rush toward him. Maybe I'm wrong. Maybe he's not faking. Maybe he can be shaded.

I hover above him, holding out my hands in front of me, unsure where to touch. 'Will.' His name escapes in a hush. As if I were afraid to say it aloud. As if giving voice to the name would make his being here untrue—make him vanish in a puff of smoke, into the mists that enclose us. As so much of me has vanished since returning here.

In the gloom, his eyes snap open. I jerk back, startled. He smiles those well-carved lips at me. Lips whose shape and texture are permanently imprinted on my memory.

I gasp, relieved, and say his name again, firmer this time. 'Will.'

He stands in one easy move, with none of the lingering effects of someone shaded, confirming that I'm right. His draki blood has left him immune.

He moves toward me, and I meet him halfway—but then I recall myself and what I need to do. I quickly step back before we can come together. Holding up a hand to ward him off, I demand in a whisper, 'What are you doing here?'

'Looking for you.' The sound of his voice makes me tremble. The velvet rumble sends shivers along my skin and tells me everything I already know. He hasn't forgotten me. He still wants me. I swallow down the thick lump in my throat.

It's the same. The way it's always been around him. The idea of forgetting him and putting him out of my life is easier when I'm not confronted with him.

'You shouldn't have come. You risk too much.'

'Jacinda.' He looks at me like I've lost my mind. 'It's me.' He seizes my hand, tugs me forward.

And I can't *not* have this. Wrong or right, selfish or not. I'll take this. Steal a moment with him. If only that. I'll make it last. Make it enough.

He hauls me into his arms and holds me so tightly I wonder if he might not crack a rib. I look up into the shadow of his face and crave to see more of him, more than what the muted moonlight reveals to me.

But I can't. This will have to be enough.

I press a palm to his cheek, savor the scratch of bristle. My heart swells at the sensation of him, the simple touch of his flesh against my hand. Something I never thought to feel again.

'You remembered me,' I whisper, searching his glowing eyes in the dark. 'You remembered that night—'

'When everyone woke up confused, I figured out what happened. I remembered you telling me about Nidia and figured that's what Tamra became. So I pretended I was just as confused as everyone else.' He laughed once, the sound a rough scrape on the air. 'My cousins still don't know what the hell happened to them. All they can guess is that someone slipped them a roofie.'

'Only you can remember?'

Relief slumps my shoulders as Will nods.

'Yeah. That night is a complete blank to them.'

To them. I stare at the shape of him in the deep gloom, at the gleam of his eyes as I let it sink in why only Will is so special.

The blood.

'It's because you're like us,' I murmur.

'What?' He tenses against me and something vibrates in his voice that tells me he understands my meaning. More than he would like.

I suck in a breath, force it down my too-tight throat. 'Well, you're enough like us apparently. A shader's talent doesn't work on other draki. You must have been transfused with enough draki blood to form a resistance to being shaded. That would explain how you're so connected to us . . . so good at tracking us. You're like us.'

We say nothing for a long moment, and I wonder if he's thinking what I am.

How else is he different? How else is he not like humans? How else is he like me? Like a draki?

I shake my head. It's too much to contemplate. And there's no way to know. Not right now. I don't know if it's something we'll ever know. But then it doesn't matter, does it? Because we only have now. For us, there will be no tomorrow. No future.

'Does it disgust you?' he asks. 'Do *I*?'

I know what he's asking, but the answer isn't simple. 'I know you didn't make any of it happen, and you're alive as a result . . . but stolen blood flows through you. Draki were butchered . . . for you.'

'I know.' In the dark, his gleaming eyes don't even blink. 'I can't deny anything that you're saying. I didn't know what my father was doing to me until it was over. You know that, right? You've got to believe that.'

'I do.'

His breath falls heavily. 'Sometimes, at night, I *feel* them. In my dreams.'

I squeeze my eyes shut for a brief moment and have

to give voice to that gnawing fear inside me. 'Is my father one of—'

'No! It's not possible. Don't think it for a second. We only started hunting this area a little over a year ago.'

Relief ripples through me. 'You could never disgust me, Will. I care about you too much.'

His hand moves along my spine and I shiver, recalling myself, and what I've come here to do.

'How'd you find me?' I ask, stalling, telling myself to pull away, to untangle myself from the wondrous feel of his arms around me. To disengage before it becomes too hard.

Too hard? I almost laugh. It's already too hard.

'This is the third time I've been out here looking for you,' he admits.

'By yourself?' I tense and glance into the thick shadows, almost as if I expect a hunter to appear there.

'I'm alone now,' he assures me. 'I came last time with my family. I slipped away while they . . .'

'Hunted,' I supply, my voice hard.

I shiver at the thought of hunters in these woods. So near the township. Now they have faces. They're no longer the hazy bogeymen of nightmares. I can see them. His father. His uncles. His cousins, Xander and Angus. They were here. Recently.

I shake my head, anger rising in me that he dared to come back. He risked so much. And not just himself. He put every life in my pride in jeopardy. 'It's too dangerous for you to be here. You shouldn't have come. If they knew who you were tonight . . .'

I shake my head. Losing him because I can't see him again is one thing, but losing him because he's gone, killed by my brethren . . .

That, I couldn't handle. It would destroy me.

'I just looked like some guy hiking the mountain.'

'Tamra and Cassian recognized you.'

'And they said nothing.'

I nod. 'For me. They kept silent for me. I promised I would get you to persuade your family to stop hunting this area.' I inhale a deep breath. 'And I promised I would make sure you never came back here again—'

'You promised *that*?' His voice lashes me. 'To who? Cassian? I'm not surprised he wanted to make sure I never come near you again.'

I want to deny that, want to say that Cassian wants Will gone simply because it's the right thing. The safe thing. It's not about jealousy or possession.

Closing my eyes in an agonized blink, I say nothing. A short time ago, Cassian was holding me like Will holds me now. I let him hold me. Kiss me.

With a choked sound, I pull away from Will, feeling like a traitor. Even if it was the loneliness, my own vulnerability that drove me into Cassian's arms . . . I *liked* it.

Will pulls me back. 'What do *you* want? You want me to leave and never come back?'

I go unresisting into his arms. I'm too weak. I've missed him too much. I thought I could put him behind me, find a future within the pride and while that prospect killed a part of me, this, right now, might be worse. Holding him, smelling his familiar scent, having him for a short time and then saying goodbye all over again. It's a dive right back into hell.

I peer through the dark, feast on what I can see of his face. The aching beauty of him. The deeply set eyes beneath dark brows. The hair that constantly rebels, falling over his forehead, begging for my hand to brush it back. His mouth, his lips.

I commit it all to memory, determined to imprint him on my soul for those quiet moments alone, in the dark, when I can reflect.

His fingers flex on my arms. 'So you're giving up on us, Jacinda?'

I search his face in the shadows. 'It's dangerous. Not just for us. For others, too. Countless lives.'

His hands slide up my arms to my face and it's too much. His broad palms. His strong fingers so tender as they hold me. My eyes burn. I blink them fiercely in an attempt to dry them.

'Where's your faith?' His thumbs gently press into my cheeks. 'We can figure out a way.'

I shake my head. 'You don't know what it's been like.'

'Did they hurt you?' His voice takes on an edge, and his hands tighten slightly. 'When you came back, did they—'

'No,' I say quickly. 'I'm fine. Not that I don't deserve punishment. Will, I revealed myself to hunters.'

'Let's make it just you and me then. No pride. No hunters. We don't have to risk anyone else.'

'What are you saying?'

'Run away with me.'

12

For a moment, as I absorb what he's saying, I let hope weave its way into my pounding heart. Me. Will. And nothing else. 'How? Where would we go?'

'Anywhere.'

I deflate inside. I thought he might have an actual plan. Thought there might be a chance. 'It's just a dream, Will.' I stroke his cheek. 'A beautiful dream.'

He jerks from my touch as if unwilling to take my comfort if it comes with a rejection. 'It doesn't have to be. It can be real, Jacinda. Come with me. Make it real.'

Frustration rises in me at being fed such an impossible hope. 'How?' I demand. 'Where would we go? How would we live?'

'My grandmother. She would help us, put us up for a little while.'

I blink. 'Your grandmother?' This is the first I've heard of a grandmother, but then Will and I still didn't know a lot of things about each other. We know the big things. The secrets. The little stuff sort of got lost within all of that, and my heart aches for all the small things waiting to be discovered if we could just be together. If we just had the time, the chance . . . if we just led normal and uncomplicated lives.

'We wouldn't stay with her forever. My dad would eventually guess where I went and come after me, but she would give us some money to get started on our own—'

I shake my head, still trying to wrap my thoughts around what he's saying. 'Why would your grandmother help us and not tell your dad?'

'She's my mom's mother and not exactly a fan of my dad. After Mom died, Dad never let her see me. He said she was too nosy. And when I was sick . . .' His features tighten. 'Well, he wouldn't let her come around.'

I hear what he's *not* saying. Will's dad didn't want his mother-in-law hanging around while he was infusing Will with draki blood.

A pang fills me, thinking how Will must have needed her growing up, a connection to the mother he lost. And then when he became sick, all he had was his dad, who isn't exactly a warm and fuzzy guy. I picture Will's young boy's face, and something cracks loose inside me.

That loneliness within him speaks to me, finds the place inside me that mirrors his wounds.

'She's not too far—in Big Sur.'

'I can't,' I say, but the words stick, taste awful in my mouth.

'You mean you won't,' he accuses. 'Is it Cassian? Have you two . . .'

'No,' I snap. 'It's not like that, Will. He's been a good friend to me when so few are right now.'

'A friend. Right. I'm sure that's all he wants from you.'

'Well, that's all *I* want.' My face burns as I recall the kiss. A kiss that was a momentary lapse on my part, a betrayal to everyone, really. Will. Tamra. Even Cassian. Even me.

He drops his face until our foreheads touch. 'So you don't want Cassian . . . and you still want me to just disappear from your life?' he whispers.

This time I can only nod against him. It hurts too much to utter the lie. Being with him—right now—is the most alive I've felt since returning here. Since I fooled myself into thinking I could ever forget him.

As if he senses me weakening, he slides his hands farther along my cheeks, fingers delving deeply into my hair, playing softly with the waves. 'Are you ready to give up on us? You really want me to walk down that mountain and never come back? To forget about you?'

At the stark rasp of his voice, at the scenario his words paint, I tremble. *No. No, I don't want that. But it has to be that way* . . .

'Tell me, Jacinda. Tell me that and I'll go. Is that what you want? To never see me again?'

A sob chokes in my throat, betrays my resolve. 'No. No.'

Then he's kissing me. Deep and hungry. His hands bury in my hair.

His lips feel cool, a shock against the perpetual heat of my own. The scald simmers at my core, and I hold myself utterly still. Sensations overwhelm me. He wakens everything in me I've been trying so hard to suppress, and I respond, kissing back with equal fervor, an animal starved. For him.

Sudden conviction races through me, almost terrifying in its total certainty.

I can't give him up.

He's the other part of me. He gets what it feels like to be separate from everything and everyone, to reject the path others lay out for you. We're the same. Two sides to the same coin.

He comes up for air long enough to whisper against my ear. 'We'll figure out a way . . .' A shudder racks me. He kisses me there, and I'm clinging to him then, fire bursting inside my chest, catching in my throat. He wraps one arm around me to hold me up and stop me from falling.

Colors race, spots dancing before me in the dark as I'm swept away on the tide of *him*—lost to the magic of his mouth and hands on me.

'Tamra,' I gasp, thinking of my sister, of our newfound closeness, 'I don't know if I can leave her.'

Then something inside me turns, lifts like the flip of a lock. Tamra doesn't need me. She has a place among the pride. She has Cassian. And maybe if I left, Cassian would finally see what he has in her. Maybe I *need* to go so they can have their chance.

Mom, however, is a different situation. True, she'd be glad for me to escape the pride. She might even want to leave with me. But could I do that? Make her choose between me and Tamra? Or am I just afraid to find out she won't pick me?

'Jacinda.' Will sighs warmly against my cheek as if he can read my thoughts. 'Just think about it. That's all I'm asking . . .'

For now. He didn't say it, but I hear it. He isn't going to give up on me. He wants us to be together. No matter how I may try to push him away.

Elation burns through me. I revel in it and nod slowly. 'I need some time.'

'Let's meet again. Two weeks.'

My breath catches. Two weeks. So long. And then I remember that it takes serious maneuvering for him to travel here. It can't be easy for him to disappear from his family without alerting them to what he's doing.

Still, the fact that Will is leaving me again sinks down on me heavily. Two weeks feels like a lifetime. I swallow thickly, cling tighter to his shirt, pulling it from his warm chest.

He glances around us at the murky little glade where we stand. 'Same spot, Ok?'

It's a solution. For now. No decision needed yet, but the promise of seeing Will again is there. I'll have *this* again—his hands on my face, the taste of him on my lips.

It's enough. Enough to keep me going for two more weeks.

'Ok,' I agree shakily, not wanting to reveal just how much I don't want him to go. He'll see that I'm weak and try to persuade me to go with him this very instant. And I can't do that as much as it tempts me.

'We're all set then.' I hear the confidence in his voice. He thinks the next time I meet him here it will be to run away with him.

And maybe it will.

'Noon,' I say. It will be riskier sneaking away during the day, but at least then I'll see the flash of his eyes shift from gold to green to brown. I'll see the burnished brown of his hair. I long for that.

'I'll be here.'

'Me too.' Somehow. Nothing could keep me away. And maybe that's my answer to the decision I'll eventually have to make.

If I can't stand to live without him, what choice is there?

113

13

I crouch just outside the township, hiding in tall summer grass and gathering my nerve as I stare at the lone shape standing sentry at the entrance. Cassian had distracted him earlier so that I could slip past.

I gnaw on the edge of my thumb, thinking about what Cassian had said about getting back into the township. *It won't be a problem. The guard won't want the pride to know that he let you sneak past him earlier.*

Hoping he's right about that, I stand and walk with sure strides toward the arched entry. If not a hundred per cent confident then I at least do a good job faking it.

'Hey, Levin,' I say, my voice easy and casual. 'What's up?'

Levin jerks up straight at the sound of my voice, his vibrant aqua-blue eyes widening. 'Jacinda! What are you—' His bright gaze swings behind him guiltily, as if Severin himself were there to witness his failure. In a much lower voice, he sputters, 'What are you doing outside the walls?'

I push my hands deeper into my jeans pockets. 'Just taking a walk.' I rock on the balls of my feet. 'Like you were doing earlier. Right? When you were supposed to be standing guard.'

Even in the dark, with the wet mist swirling around us in teasing tendrils, I make out the ruddy flush to his features. 'Um, yeah.'

'Look. It's no big deal.' I shrug. 'I mean, I'm not going to say anything . . .' I let my voice fade, the implication clear.

'Yeah,' he says quickly. 'Me either. Go.' He motions behind him. 'Go on.'

Smiling, I walk past him. 'Thanks.'

Near Nidia's house, I hesitate, the smile slipping from my mouth. The windows are lightless. Nidia and Tamra are both probably exhausted, passed out after their shading efforts on Will today.

I glance to the sky, imagine my sister as I saw her, cutting through the solid night, euphoric at what's still so new and wondrous to her.

A sound emerges on the eerie quiet of the night. Gravel crunches beneath the weight of someone's feet. My pulse jumps against my neck. I pause, at first thinking that Levin changed his mind and followed me, determined to turn me in.

Pasting a smile to my lips, I whirl around, ready to persuade him again to forget that he'd seen me sneaking back into the township.

But he's not there.

Frowning, I spot Levin's hazy figure still at the guardhouse in the distance. I turn in a full circle, peering deeply into the gray curls of fog rolling around me like an endless tide. Vapor sticks to my skin in a thin sheen of moisture.

But no one's there.

The wind shifts, and the mist blows the other way. The wisps framing my face stir, tickle my cheeks.

Snap.

Expecting to see someone at last, I spin in the direction of the cracking twig, long strands of hair striking me in the face.

'Hello?' My voice rings out on the night. 'Who's there?'

Glaring through air that shivers like smoke, I wait for a member of the patrol to step forward, but no one does. Heat swells beneath my tightening skin, my fight-or-flight instinct kicking in. A patrol wouldn't hide their presence.

Still, the sensation that I'm not alone persists.

Hugging myself, I chafe my hands over my arms. Turning back around, I head down the path, cutting quickly through the evening fog, eager to reach my house.

I'm almost to the center of town, when a voice breaks through the sound of my footfalls.

'Hey.'

I jerk to a stop, turn, and watch as Cassian materializes from the mists.

'Have you been following me through town?' I demand. 'Why didn't you say something?'

'What?' He frowns. 'No, I've been waiting here.'

I stare at him suspiciously, casting another glance over my shoulder as if I'd find someone there, lurking, watching me.

I turn back around as Cassian asks, 'Did you do it? Did you tell him to never come back?'

'Yeah. I told him.' I did. At least at first.

Lowering my gaze, I resume my pace, crossing my arms in front of me.

116

He falls into step beside me. 'You Ok?'

'I'll be fine.' I shake my head. 'It's been . . . a lot today.'

'I know it has.' He stops and faces me, both hands on my shoulders. 'You did the right thing.'

The right thing. I don't know what that is anymore. A lump clogs my throat. I can't speak, can't utter another lie. I just nod jerkily. Shrugging from his grasp, I turn, eager to be away from him. His presence twists me into knots . . . fills me with guilt. About the kiss. About the lies I've told him tonight. About the possibility of leaving the pride forever and undoing his trust in me.

He keeps pace with me, and I slide a glance at him, desperately wanting to be alone right now.

He seems to understand. 'I'll walk you home so you won't get cited if we're stopped. I can tell them I was escorting you to check on Tamra or something.'

It's with these words that I know what my life would be like if I stayed here. It wouldn't be a *bad* life. Cassian would always be my friend, would always have my back, and he would help me regain acceptance among the pride. And I eventually would—*if* I could do my part.

If I could forget Will.

If I could pretend I wasn't miserable inside. It's all up to me.

I brush my fingers to my lips where I can still feel him. Somehow I don't think I can ever forget. These last weeks, I'd convinced myself that I could put him behind me . . . that I *had*. Tonight proved me wrong. He's always been here. He always will.

* * *

117

Days later I stand at my mother's door, knocking gently. 'Mom,' I call.

The low sound of her television carries through the door. Her shift ended hours ago, so I know she's been home for a while. She's probably hungry. I didn't see any dishes in the sink.

With another knock, I push open the door and enter the dim room. She lies on the bed in her bathrobe, her stare fixed on the television. I blink at the unmade bed. Mom always makes the bed. I've never seen it unmade this late in the day before.

A half-full glass of verda wine sits on the nightstand. Beside the glass stands the bottle. Of late the wine is all that sustains her. Not much as far as sustenance goes. I wonder why they haven't stopped her from taking so much of it home from the clinic. It's used mostly for curative purposes, not for open consumption.

'Hey, Mom.'

She flicks her attention away from the rerun of a sitcom. 'Hi, Jace. Have a good day?' Her eyes are dull and lifeless.

The question is merely rote. Something to say.

And how should I respond to a mother who's checked out? Is there anything I can say—*do*—to bring her back to me?

'Fine. Good.' I clear my throat, determined to do everything I can to revive her. How can I leave her like this? If I run away with Will, who's going to take care of her? 'They're playing jako at the rec tonight. The tournament was interrupted last night. Thought you might like to go and watch—maybe play.'

'No,' she says quickly. 'I don't feel like being around a crowd.'

Of course, I think. All you've done is show up to work, occasionally visit Tamra, and drink yourself to sleep every night. Socializing among the pride who's taken your daughters from you would not be your idea of a good time.

'Well, we could have a girls' night in,' I suggest. 'How about I cook?'

Her gaze flits over me and I wonder if she's realizing that she hasn't cooked in over a week.

'Sure,' she murmurs, but the word is dragged out, reluctant, and I know. She doesn't want company. Not even mine.

Pasting a smile to my face, I pretend that I don't notice her reluctance. 'Great. I'll let you know when dinner's ready.' I gently close the door behind me and head into the kitchen.

As I fill up a pot of water, I hear a sound. A creaking floorboard.

I turn quickly. 'Mom?'

Nothing.

Then I hear it again, another creaky board. I take a few steps into the living room.

'Hello?' I wait several moments, staring out at the empty room. Shaking my head, I turn into the kitchen, rubbing at the prickly flesh at the back of my neck. It's not the first time I've thought I heard someone in the house. I sigh, figuring it's no surprise I'm so jumpy with everything that's happened over the last couple months.

My thoughts turn back to Mom, and anger bubbles up inside me at her total lack of interest in . . . *anything*. The defiant thought skitters through my head that I shouldn't even bother letting her know when dinner's ready. But then that anger diminishes and I just feel sad. Because she wouldn't even care.

My mom has vanished from me. It's not even her in that room. It's her ghost, and I know I have to at least try and get her back. That I can't consider leaving until I do.

I spot Az through my living room window. I've only seen her at school, and she's usually with someone else. The need to talk with her alone, before I see Will again and possibly leave the pride for good surges inside me.

Snatching up my shoes, I sit on the couch and fumble with the laces, determined to end this distance between us. I miss her and want things right.

The knock at the door makes my heart jump. *Az.* Apparently I won't have to chase her down the street. She's come to me.

Prepared to grovel, I open the door quickly, hoping Az has had a change of heart and that's why she's here. After all, we've had our fights before, but nothing like this. She can't stay mad at me forever.

Only it's not Az on my front porch.

'Jacinda.' A corner of Cassian's mouth lifts as he says my name. It's one of those rare smiles of his and it affects me as it shouldn't. I fidget, shifting on my feet. I don't want this. Don't want *him*. Maybe if my sister wasn't totally in love with him. Maybe before Will came back I was weak enough to embrace Cassian and all his half smiles. Not now. Now I want more.

I want Will.

I shake my head as Cassian walks inside my house. So much for catching Az alone. I look out the door and see her figure, small in the distance. Shutting the door, I cross my arms and face him.

His shadow falls over me, encroaching, close. I'm root-
ed to the spot. Despite everything I can't seem to move.
'What do you want?'

He doesn't speak. Just stands so close, his eyes scour-
ing, delving so deeply into me, tricking me again into
thinking he sees me. The real me beneath everything.
Beneath the girl. Beneath the draki. Past the bones and
flesh and smolder. And yet if he really did see me, then he
would have known I couldn't have said goodbye to Will.
He would know I lied to him. He would know I struggle
with facing him now, my deceit an ugly thing between
us.

My gaze stops on his mouth, the lips that kissed mine.
My stare lingers there until my chest grows tight, breath
constricted. He lifts his hand and I flinch.

Feeling foolish, I hold my ground as his thumb grazes
my cheek.

'What are you doing?' I whisper.

'Touching you.'

The pads of his fingers slide across my jaw, over my
bottom lip, so soft, coaxing, and I know what he wants. I
feel it in his touch. See it in the way his dark eyes devour
me. He breathes my name.

For one second, I lean in, and then suddenly I'm
springing away from Cassian.

It's not a sudden surge of conscience that tears us apart.
It's a gasp. And I know we're not alone.

14

I spin and lock gazes with my sister. Her face is flushed, her cheeks a ruddy color that looks almost obscene on her alabaster skin.

My skin goes cold then hot. 'Tamra.' I barely hear myself say her name, just feel it rise up in my throat in a pained whimper. Her frosty pale eyes flit back and forth between me and Cassian.

'What?' she challenges, her voice hard, cruel, so at odds with the way she looks—shaken and fragile, even more unearthly pale than usual. 'What is it? What's so damn special about her?' She looks only at Cassian as she demands this. 'Tell me!'

'Nothing,' I start to say. 'Nothing, Tam—'

She swings on me. 'I'm talking to Cassian, Jacinda!' Her attention returns to him. 'I mean, I really want to know. We have the same face!' She bites off these words with a snarl. 'Well, mostly.' She tosses back a lock of silvery hair. 'And now I'm not only a true draki, but I have a talent that rivals Jacinda's. So what is it?' Her pale gaze glimmers with hot emotion, searching his face, desperate and hungry for an answer.

Cassian stands there for a long moment. I suffer in silence, wait for him to tell her there's nothing special about me, that it's just habit that keeps him coming back to me.

Tamra shakes her head slowly. 'Just tell me.' Her next question comes out small, a weak whisper that makes my heart twist in pain. 'Why not me?'

Cassian replies finally, his voice low and anguished. 'I don't know. I've tried . . . since we've come back, I've tried . . . But you're just not her.'

His words do something inside me that I wished they didn't. For a moment I let warmth curl around my heart. Let myself believe that I'm special to him. That I'm more than the fire-breather he was *taught* to prefer.

Tamra looks as if she suffered a blow. Faint splotches of red stain the pale curve of her throat. 'Yeah? Too bad she doesn't feel the same way. It will never be you, you know. Not for her. Think about that. When she's with you it will be *him* she's missing.'

Then she's gone. Out the door fast.

I stare at the spot where she stood a moment ago. 'Why did you do that?'

'Spoke the truth, you mean?'

'The truth? I thought the two of you—'

'No,' he says simply, bluntly, shaking his dark head. 'I tried . . . but I can't.'

I close my eyes in a long-suffering blink. Opening them, I face him. 'She's right. It will always be Will.'

'No,' he refutes again with infuriating confidence. 'He was your escape. When you stop running, you'll see it's me you belong with. I might have doubted it before, but then you kissed me in the tower—'

'That,' I say sharply, 'was a mistake. A serious lapse in judgment.'

'Maybe Will's the mistake.'

I pull back at that.

'Let's pretend for one moment that you could get your precious Will. That you give up your pride, your family, your life to be with him. You don't think one day you would wake up and look at him and realize he's just some hunter with blood on his hands? A hunter with *stolen* blood in his veins?'

I shake my head. 'No! I don't want to hear this—'

'Because it's true. You think you can live with that? When the fantasy wears off, when the first thrilling rush of being with him fades . . . you'll remember just why it is he's wrong for you.'

'I don't know why we're even talking about this. I'm never going to see him again,' I say, my voice shaking at the lie.

He stares at me so intently I fear he detects my deceit. 'I just don't want any misunderstanding between us anymore,' he says firmly.

'I understand the situation perfectly. You and I aren't going to happen.' I motion toward the door. 'You really should go after Tamra. She's upset.'

'And I'm sorry for that.' He inhales, his broad chest lifting high. 'But I'm not sorry about us.'

'There is no *us*,' I hiss, clenching my hands into fists.

He moves for the door, his stride easy and relaxed. 'I can be patient. We have time.' Then he's gone, the door gaping open after him.

Time is the last thing I have here. Soon, I'll meet with Will. *And I'll leave with him.* I reach this decision with blinding-bright clarity. Any lingering doubt I have about that is completely gone.

After my shift the following day, I head for Az's house on the opposite end of the township. I have to see her. I have to make things right before I leave. As much as I can, anyway.

She opens the door for me. With an arched eyebrow, she stares for a long moment before motioning me inside with an elegant flick of her hand.

She soundlessly marches up the stairs to her room, her long blue-streaked hair swishing fluidly down her back. At the bottom of the stairs, I get sidetracked when her mom spots me as she comes out of the kitchen.

'Jacinda!' Sobha pulls me into a hug. I don't hug her back right away, too surprised. I'd forgotten how nice it felt to have another pride member show me such warmth. 'It's about time you came around. I remember when you were here practically every other night.'

I remember those days, too. After I manifested and Tamra failed to do so, my friendship with Az grew even more. We were inseparable.

'Mom,' Az calls down.

'Oh, I won't keep you.' She pats me fondly on the shoulder. 'Go on up.'

Az's room is everything I remember. Bright pinks and blues, posters of the ocean. I approach one shot of Carmel beach. As girls we would talk about taking our tours together and going there. Back when I thought the pride would allow me to go. Now I realize that was always unlikely. They valued me too greatly to ever risk losing me, and everyone knew that draki sometimes never returned from their tours.

Still, we dreamed, believing when we were eighteen it would be our time. Our turn. Like so many draki before us, we would venture out and live for a year among humans, learning the ways of the outside world before returning to the pride.

Smiling, I brush a palm against the glossy-cool paper. The beach set against the verdant hillside looks like something out of an Italian travel brochure. Maybe Az would still get to swim beneath those cerulean blue waters in full manifest. Only without me.

I drop down on her bed, plucking a fuzzy heart-shaped pillow from the mound at the top of the bed. I hug it to my chest. 'I've missed this room.'

She stands at her window, her pose stiff, her thin arms crossed over her chest. 'Yeah,' she says crossly. 'I wouldn't have guessed that.'

'I miss *you*,' I add, determined to get to the point. I don't have time for much else.

'You have a funny way of showing it. You went off and—'

'I didn't choose to leave here,' I insert, but she ignores me and keeps talking.

'And fell for some human. You manifested in front of him.' She presses a hand to her heart. 'I can't believe you would put us all in danger like that. The Jacinda I know would never—'

'The Jacinda you know couldn't stand by and watch him die.' My fingers ache where they clutch the pillow. 'Not when I could do something about it. He fell off a

126

cliff, Az. There wasn't time to think. I just acted.' I stare hard at her, pleading, willing for her to understand.

She studies me for a long moment before asking, 'Would you have stayed there? If Cassian hadn't come for you?' Her voice is no longer angry now, just hurt, and I want to lie. I want to spare her from any pain, but I've lied enough lately.

'Yes. I think I would have.'

After a long moment, she shakes her head. With a loud sigh, she drops down beside me and gives me a playful shove. 'I hope he was hot at least.'

A smile tugs my mouth. This is the funny, quirky Az I love and remember. My smile slips and I look at her intently, willing her to never forget this moment, these words: 'He's really special, Az. That day we snuck out and the hunters chased us, he saw me; he let me go. He's the reason I escaped. He cares about me for me. Not because of what I am.' I laugh hoarsely. 'I've never been able to say that about any other guy.' Although lately, the way Cassian looks at me—no, I shove that thought away. I'm leaving with Will.

She stares down at her hands and nods slowly. 'I guess I can understand that.'

'I need you to,' I whisper fervently. 'I really need you to.'

She lifts her gaze to mine, and I read the silent question in her eyes. A question I won't answer. When they come to her, I want her to look them in the face and tell them in all honesty that she knew nothing of my plans.

'I do,' she finally says.

I can't stop myself then. I pull her close for a hug. Squeezing her, I say, 'Thanks.' My voice catches and she smooths her hand down my hair.

'Hey. It's OK. I'm not mad anymore. When have I ever been able to stay mad at you? I think this was definitely a record.'

I start to laugh and the sound turns into a wet hiccup. 'Just remember that next time I tick you off.'

'Planning a next time already?' she teases.

Something tightens in my chest. 'Just in case,' I hedge.

'Oh, Jacinda.' She shakes her head at me. 'So doom and gloom. Don't worry about what hasn't even happened. Just live in the moment.'

I sniffle and swipe a hand at my nose. 'I am.' My gaze sweeps the room, searching, the tightness in my chest easing when I spot what I'm looking for on her desk. 'Now. How about a game of cards?'

I stay at Az's until her mom comes in and warns me that it's twenty minutes until curfew. With a hurried goodbye and a promise to see her tomorrow, I leave, my heart lighter to have made amends with Az. Hopefully she'll remember tonight and understand when she hears that I've gone.

When I arrive home, I head down the hall, eager for a shower. Bumping into my sister coming out of her room is the last thing I expect.

'Tamra, I didn't know you were coming over.'

Her face doesn't crack an expression and it's so reminiscent of when we were kids—when she would get really mad at me and try to look so very stern—that I have to fight back a smile. 'It's still my house, Jacinda. I grew up here.'

'Of course.'

The awkward moment stretches between us as we stand in the tight space of the corridor. She finally breaks the silence by motioning behind her to her door. 'I needed to get a few things.'

I nod, having nothing to say . . . everything to say. And yet words fail me.

She starts to move past me, and I watch her, my heart in my throat, thinking of the horrible scene with Cassian. And yet it only confirms that leaving Tamra might be the best thing for her, might give her just what she needs. A life where she's able to shine in her own light. Without me to share it.

She turns as if struck with a thought. 'I checked in on Mom. What's going on? She doesn't look good.'

'She's not,' I answer matter-of-factly before I can think about candy-coating the truth. When I go, Tamra better know about what's going on with Mom. Mom's going to need her. They'll need each other. 'They're working her long hours. Punishing her, I guess.'

Tamra's voice comes out weakly. 'I didn't know.'

'You might have some pull now. Maybe you can get them to lay off her a little.'

She nods. 'I'll try.'

'And she's drinking too much, sneaking verda wine from the clinic . . .'

'That doesn't sound like her.'

I don't like the accusation I hear in her voice. Like I'm either lying or I'm the reason our mother has taken solace in a bottle. 'I've been trying to get her to eat at least. But she's had a rough time over the last few weeks. She's depressed.'

'Why haven't you told me any of this?'

'You haven't asked.'

She blinks and I know I've stung her. Maybe unfairly. Tamra didn't ask for what happened to her, after all. She didn't ask to move in with Nidia and leave Mom. She's just trying to cope. Like I am. 'Look,' I say, 'just don't forget about her. She needs you.' *Because I won't be here.*

Tamra stares at me curiously before nodding slowly. She moves for the door. Her hand is on the knob when I hear myself blurt, 'I'm sorry, Tamra.'

She looks over her shoulder. One glimpse into her eyes and I know she understands what I'm talking about. It's been there between us since I walked into the house. *Cassian.*

'For what? Being what he wants?'

'I'm not,' I insist. 'He just doesn't know it.'

'And he never will.' She doesn't sound angry as she says this. Simply tired, defeated. She reminds me a bit of Mom in that moment, or at least what Mom's become lately. Again, I can't help wondering whether my leaving might be the best thing for both of them. Having me around hasn't made life easy for either of them.

'Goodnight, Tam,' I say, but what I really hear myself saying is *goodbye*. Soon I'll be gone.

'Night, Jace.' With a nod, my sister leaves the house.

15

After Tamra leaves, I shower and change into pajama
bottoms and a tank top. The television flickers blue
light down the hall from Mom's room.

As I walk the darkened hallway, the wood floor
creaks beneath my feet. I have a flash of me, years ago,
tiptoeing down the same hall into my parents' room.
Never Tamra. Just me. I would crawl carefully across
the cool sheets of their bed and sandwich myself between them, feeling so safe and loved with their arms
wrapped around me.

In the morning, I would always wake to a lecture
about needing to be a big girl and sleeping in my own
bed. And yet a few days later, I would find my way back
to my parents' room. They never turned me away.

I glance around that bedroom now, Mom all alone in
that great big bed. I always felt at peace here, with them
in that bed. Nothing could touch me then.

I move to turn off the television.

'It's all my fault.'

I freeze at the sound of Mom's voice. Her tone is so soft; I inch closer to the bed. 'What, Mom?'

'None of this would have happened if it wasn't for me.' Her gaze fixes blindly on the television without glancing my way. 'I should have taken you anywhere, but I took you there.'

At first I don't understand. 'Where?'

'Because I was selfish and wanted to remember . . .'

'Remember what?'

'Your father.' She turns her face into the pillow then, muffling the sound of what I suspect are tears. This shakes me. I can't remember Mom crying. Not even when Dad went missing.

'Chaparral. It was the only place your father and I ever had together. Even if just for a few days, before he persuaded me to come back here. It was just the two of us there. No pride. Just us in the desert sky.'

I resist telling her that they didn't go unnoticed. At least she hadn't. She'd been spotted flying. It was because of her that Will's family moved there. While most people dismissed a draki sighting as some weird bird, or a contrived device—an alleged UFO—others took note. Hunters paid attention to such reports.

But I can't blame her. I understand what it's like to take risks for someone you love . . . to break rules to be with someone you love. I angle my head, studying my mother. I always thought I was like Dad but maybe I'm more my mother's daughter than I ever realized.

'It's not your fault,' I say, turning off the television and moving to tuck the covers around her that she's kicked off.

She settles back to sleep without a sound. After a moment of staring down at her shadowy figure, I slip into bed beside her, beneath the cool, familiar sheets. I position myself close, so that I feel her warmth.

Sliding a hand between my cheek and a pillow, I close my eyes and reach for the peace I once found here.

Even though I made up my mind days ago, my hand shakes as I sign my name to the letter. This is it. There's no going back from this moment. After carefully folding the paper four ways, I place it on the pillow beside the first note I wrote. I figured Mom and Tamra each deserve their own letter.

For a second, I hear the creak of a floorboard and stiffen, looking over my shoulder, afraid Mom is back from work early. I stare at the open door of my room and wait several moments, but nothing. Not a sound. Sighing, I return my attention to the letters, hoping that constant unease, the sense that I am always watched, will abandon me once I'm gone from here.

Both notes are brief, to the point. I tell Mom and Tamra how much I love them. How much I will miss them. I ask them not to worry about me, that I'm seizing my own happiness, and I hope they will do the same.

Eyes burning, I smooth a hand over the letters, the paper crinkling beneath my fingers. I don't specify where I'm going—or with whom. But they will know. They'll read between the lines. And I hope they understand. Straightening, I grab my backpack from the floor. With a quick glance around my childhood room, I leave it all behind.

'Where you headed in such a rush?' For a moment I consider pretending I don't hear Corbin behind me. I'd managed to avoid him lately. 'Jacinda! Wait up.'

Sighing, I stop. I should at least look like I'm trying to assimilate back into pride life and talk to him. Instead of hurrying off to escape, like I am.

I face Corbin. 'To Nidia's.'

'Tamra's not there. She's working out on the flight field. We can join her if you want.'

'I'm not in the mood,' I reply and turn, continuing toward Nidia's. It's almost noon.

Only Corbin doesn't go away.

I realize I might actually *have* to go inside Nidia's house to back up my claim if he doesn't leave. Not that I have a plan on how I'm going to get past the guard on duty, anyway. I'm just trusting that a solution will present itself.

'You want to go to the rec later?' Corbin asks, like this might be a possibility. Like I've softened toward him.

'No, thanks.'

'Jacinda, when are you going to quit playing so hard to get?'

I keep walking, my annoyance evident with every jarring step. 'I'm not *playing* anything.'

'Well, you're going to be paired with someone eventually.'

My skin tightens, prickles at this. Because he's probably right. The pride won't allow me to remain mate-less for many more years. Either I choose someone—Severin approved, of course—or I'll be assigned to someone. All the more reason to put as much distance between myself and the pride.

'Cassian isn't going to—'

'I don't care about Cassian,' I snap, hating the surge of heat in my face at the obvious lie.

He's been in my head ever since I returned here, right there beside Will.

I misjudged Cassian. He doesn't want me because I'm the pride's coveted fire-breather. It's not like I've always thought. Otherwise, he would want Tamra, my twin, now a draki of equal, if not higher, status.

Impossible as it seems, Cassian wants me. For *me*.

The realization only infuriates me. My heart belongs to Will. I don't need Cassian complicating things . . . making hard what should be easy. Why couldn't he just want Tamra?

Thoughts of Will and Cassian have tangled together like strings hopelessly knotted. Only today that ends. Today I choose.

Corbin stops. I stop, too, and look him in the face with all the coldness I feel in my heart when I gaze upon him.

'Good to hear you don't care about Cassian,' he announces. 'That means there's nothing in our way.'

I shake my head. 'Look, Corbin, you and I aren't going to happen. Ever.'

'We'll see,' he murmurs with a sly smile, like he knows something I don't. He flicks a glance over my shoulder, as though he sees something there. I follow his gaze but see nothing. 'Tell Nidia hello for me.'

He leaves then and I continue toward Nidia's house, more convinced than ever that I need to leave.

The guard on duty isn't Levin this time. Unlucky for me, this one actually looks like he's taking his job seriously— even stares hard at me as I knock on Nidia's door, my mind feverishly working at a plan to get past him and meet Will.

I knock again. No answer. Feeling his gaze on me, I casually turn down the street like I'm heading back to the center of town. Once I'm far enough away that he can't see me, I swing a hard left into some bushes. Heart hammering, I push through the thick foliage that backs up against several houses and loop around, coming up on the backside of Nidia's cottage.

Looking around wildly, I reassure myself that no one's nearby before quickly stripping off my clothes. With a deep breath, I let myself go.

The familiar pull begins in my chest, a tight, twisting heat. Moist air surrounds me, feeding my draki.

My human exterior fades away, buries itself as my face tightens, cheeks sharpening and stretching . . . transforming. My breathing changes, becomes deeper, hotter as ridges push out from the bridge of my nose. My muscles loosen, lengthen. I angle my face to the sky, relish the sensation of wet wind.

My wings grow. I sigh as they release themselves, unfurl with a gentle whisper on the air, enjoying the freedom. My draki skin glimmers, the fiery gold reflecting what little sunlight sifts through the afternoon mist.

Snatching my clothes, I stuff them into my backpack and stare accusingly at the ivy-tangled wall, sick of the sight of it. Tired of living in a cage. Looping the strap of my backpack around my arm, I ready myself.

In an easy move, I spring, launching myself over the perimeter wall.

Already manifested, I don't even bother landing on my feet. I plunge into the woods, cutting through the air, weaving through trees. I don't go too far. Just far enough to put the pride behind me.

With an exultant breath, I lower to the ground, luxuriating in the stretch of my wings, like two great sails behind me. Setting down on the balls of my feet, I tuck myself behind a large tree and demanifest. My wings fold together. I urge them down, draw them deep between my shoulder blades.

Heavy breath saws from my lips. Not from exhaustion. I'm built for much more exertion. This is all adrenaline. Fear and excitement course through me and simmer in my veins.

I dress quickly, stabbing my legs clumsily into my shorts, all the while listening for a distant alert . . . any indication that I'd been spotted leaving the township. Nothing.

After several moments my breathing eases. I did it. I slipped away undetected.

Hitching my backpack over one shoulder, I shove off from the tree and head for the glade. For Will.

16

Too much time has passed. I stare up at the trees, peer through the branches, and soak up the sunlight filtering down between the breaks and gaps. The paltry light settles on my human skin and sits there, flat, not like when it catches on my draki skin and shimmers like flame.

Birds chirp, talk to each other in overlapping calls. The wind whistles slow and low through the towering trees.

Will, where are you?

I hug myself, chafe my hands up and down my arms. It's been almost an hour, and still I wait, my heart sinking, despondency creeping into my heart. *He isn't coming.*

I'll be missed soon. If he's not coming . . . if I'm not leaving, then I can't stay much longer. Not unless I want to be caught.

Still, I linger, alternating between sitting, standing, and pacing the misty glade where I last saw him. Holding each other and whispering dreams and promises. Impossible dreams, but still I let myself hope.

I glance around, study the press of forest as if he'll emerge from the shadows at any moment.

I don't know quite when I notice it, but I fall still, utterly motionless. And listen.

Total silence. Unnatural.

I'm not alone. My skin ripples with awareness of this fact. Someone else has arrived. Excitement bubbles up in my chest, and I feel like I just downed one of the fizzy orange sodas Dad always bought me on our trips to town.

Will. My gaze scans the fringe of trees and brush surrounding me, hungry for the sight of him. And yet something stops me from saying his name. From calling out.

The silence hangs, swinging into this eerie, living thing, breathing menacingly all around me.

And then I realize whoever's out there—isn't Will. Will would have revealed himself by now. He wouldn't do this to me.

A sound breaks the stillness. Something wrong for the setting. No bird call, no rustle of wind through the mist-shrouded trees.

A twig cracks. Just once. As if a body moved, tested its weight, and stopped. My gaze focuses on that spot, staring hard into the dense foliage.

'Who's there?' I finally ask.

Nothing.

Countless possibilities race through my mind. Did someone follow me? Corbin? The guard? Or is it a hunter? One of Will's family?

It occurs to me that waiting to find out is a bad idea. I push into the trees, slap at branches as I head away from the glade and away from the township. Just in case it's a hunter . . . I can't lead them back there.

And there it is again. Footsteps keeping a steady pace behind mine. Gratified that I'm not paranoid, I steer my thoughts into losing whoever it is trailing me. Definitely not a friend. A friend would announce himself.

Heat swims through my skin. I walk briskly, plunging deeper into the woods. My heart pounds with every step I take.

I tromp through high grass, wondering how a day that held such promise could twist so horribly into something else. I should be in Will's arms, but instead I'm playing some sort of cat-and-mouse game. The snowcapped mountains peer down at me through the latticework of branches.

Tired of feeling like prey, I swing around abruptly. 'Come out! I know you're there.'

Silence.

I scour the trees, searching.

Then I see her. A figure steps out from behind a tree.

'Miram.' I breathe her name. I guess I should be glad she showed herself to me. She didn't have to.

'I thought you were never going to stop. What are you doing out here?' she demands, propping a fist on her hip and looking around expectantly. 'Meeting someone?'

'No,' I say quickly.

'Then why would you sneak off—'

'I just wanted some time alone.' I look her up and down. 'I guess that's not going to happen.'

She cocks her head, says lightly, blandly, 'I don't believe you.'

I try to look innocent. Hope it works. 'Why not?'

She smiles widely and pulls something from her pocket. It takes me a moment to grasp what it is she holds. *Paper.* Two folded slips of paper.

'My letters,' I say numbly. 'You went inside my house? My room?'

She flutters the letters in the air. 'Lots of times. It's amazing the things I know that no one else does. The things people leave out and about. Who wants to be a fire-breather when you can be invisible?'

Then it clicks. 'You've been spying on me!' The sounds . . . the sensation of always being watched. It wasn't my imagination. It was *her*.

She nods cheerfully, not in the least ashamed.

'Why?' I shake my head. 'Why do you hate me so much?'

Her face screws tight. 'For years I've watched the pride bow down to you; even my own family treated you like some great savior—overlooking me like I'm something lesser, of no importance. And when there's only five—' She holds up a hand, each of her fingers splayed wide. 'Five visiocrypters in the pride. We're special, too, you know.'

I sigh. 'Really? That's why you're so nasty to me? Because you don't get enough attention?'

'Oh, shut up, Jacinda. I don't know why you're acting so smug. You're a traitor. You'll never be trusted again. Why do you think my father asked me to keep an eye on you?'

'Severin put you up to this?'

She nods. 'I couldn't agree fast enough.'

I inhale, forcing myself to block out the bitter flow of her words. The only thing I can concentrate on is the sudden low drone rumbling on the air. Distant but agonizingly familiar.

The moment becomes like another one not so long ago—even if it feels like a lifetime has passed

141

since then. A lifetime since an arrow ripped through my wing. Since I was the prey, hunted down on this very mountain. A lifetime since I first saw Will. Since he spared me, *saved* me, and claimed a piece of my heart.

Except this time, the hunters are too close . . . too close to the pride. I know the township must be aware and in full-scale alert.

Miram turns her head. 'What is—'

'Sshh.' I slice a hand through the air and listen harder. The mist increases, rolls in a thick vapor at my feet and I know it's coming from Nidia.

The pride must be in lockdown, fully shrouded, buried in Nidia's mind-numbing shade. Tamra probably has a hand in it, too.

Anxiety rips through me. The choppers can see nothing of the pride from their vantage. Which means they might send in their land units to investigate the area more thoroughly.

The beating drone grows louder, closer.

Miram's eyes bulge. 'Are those helicopters?'

I nod. 'Yeah. C'mon. We have to go.' I grab her hand and pull her after me.

'Where are we going?'

'Away from the township.' I run, dragging her behind me.

'They can't see us through the trees. And the mist,' she complains. 'We're out of sight.'

I keep running, pushing harder, not bothering to tell her that where there are choppers, land units aren't far behind. I know this, have lived it firsthand.

'Jacinda, talk to me!' Panic edges her voice.

I need her calm. Easy and calm and ready to do whatever I tell her. 'It's OK, Miram,' I say. 'Just keep moving.'

'I've never been this far from the township . . . Shouldn't we be going toward home? Not away from it?'

'And lead the hunters straight to the pride?' I shake my head. 'No.'

This is all I can explain because right then I hear another sound. The rev of motors. The distant buzz growls its way toward us. My chest burns, fire eating up my windpipe.

'Jacinda!' My name explodes from her lips. She wrenches her arm free and stops, glaring at me, rubbing her wrist. 'What's going on!'

She's too loud. I grab both her arms and give her a small shake, desperate to make my point. 'Look, this isn't random aircraft.' I pause for breath. 'They're hunters. They're on the mountain looking for us.'

Her eyes grow enormous in her small face, and I realize just how young she is. Only a year younger than I am, but she seems younger. I *feel* older.

As I stare at Cassian's sister, it hits me hard. *I can't let anything happen to her. I have to protect her.* I don't let myself ponder why this is. It's just something I have to do. I have to save her, brat that she is. I have to keep her safe. For him.

'Listen to me,' I command.

And she does. Impossible as it seems, her eyes grow even bigger—more expressive than I've ever seen. Unfortunately, it's terror that I read there.

It's no surprise what happens next. Her pupils thin to vertical slits, shuddering with fear.

'Stop, Miram,' I hiss, shaking her. 'Not now.'

'I can't,' she spits, her speech garbling, altering behind her teeth.

Her draki eyes roll wild with her fear, looking everywhere, all around her, anywhere but at me. Her skin flashes, a shimmery neutral color, like milk-infused coffee. Not that different from the color of her human flesh except for the iridescent glimmer. And I know it's too late. She's lost to her instincts.

'OK, fine,' I snap, digging my fingers into her arms, and shaking her hard, snapping her gaze back to me. 'Look at me, Miram. Can you make yourself invisible?'

Instead of answering me, she releases a keening moan.

'Quiet!' Frustration boils up in me at a dark and dangerous simmer. The familiar heat sears through me.

'I don't do well under pressure,' she whines.

For a moment I want to inflict bodily harm on her.

I glance around, assessing, listening, judging how close the hunters are. The droning buzz of engines sounds closer. I glance at the trees and grimly announce, 'Strip.'

'W-what?' she asks, her voice lost to the guttural rumble of draki-speech.

'Strip. We'll hide in the trees,' I explain, my English starting to fade out, turning into a thick, garbled sound as my vocal cords alter.

I release her and tear off my clothes. My heart feels like lead in my chest, an aching weight. Here I am. Again. Running from hunters.

After a stunned moment, Miram clumsily strips; her wings, clear as glass with latticing cords the color of bone, spring free. Her fear has hold over her, and she's manifesting without thought, without deliberation, her face transforming, angles sharpening, lengthening.

I lift my chin and inhale, draw air into my seizing lungs. My skin fades, draki skin emerging in a burning rush.

I ball my clothes up with Miram's and stuff them with my backpack deep into a knot hole, hastily tossing leaves and dirt over them with shaking hands. The toxic taste of fear laces my mouth. No reason to fight it anymore.

Flinging my head back, I release a little moan as my wings push out from between my shoulder blades, the twin gossamer sheets snapping on the air. My toes lift off the ground.

How did this happen? I was supposed to see Will—be in his arms right now. How has everything gone so horribly wrong? Where's Will? Does he know what's happening? How could he let his family come up the mountain today? Today of all days?

Grabbing Miram's hand, I take off, get sucked up into wind and air. Feel the long strands of my hair lift up off my shoulders in a fiery storm.

Miram doesn't resist. She's already there, acting on instincts that demand flight, escape. I stop her, yank on her hand to keep her from ascending and soaring past the treetops into the choppers' line of vision.

Our wings smack the air, stirring leaves and making more noise than I like. I shove her into a tree and follow her in, squeezing between the jabbing branches.

Our gazes connect through the bramble of pine and twigs. She stares at me without her usual animosity. Her eyes are wild with fear, the thin sliver of her pupils shuddering with her terror. I imagine my own eyes look the same.

Crouching high in the tree, I cock my head as my hearing sharpens. I know the moment before they break through the trees that they're here, upon us—that I'll have to be as quiet and still as I've ever been if I hope to keep them from swarming over us.

17

They advance slowly, crawling really, over the forest floor like a slow-spreading infection. Once the armada of dirt bikes and various gleaming trucks and SUVs shatter into sight, I realize why they're not moving faster.

Dread sinks through me as I see that they're paying particularly close attention to the trees. The very trees where we hide.

Miram's clutch on my arm intensifies, her talons digging into my flesh, and I know she understands this, too.

I wet my lips and ask Miram as quietly as possible if she can make herself invisible. Even as quiet as I am, I wince at the guttural rumble of my question.

I know she can. She's a visiocrypter. That's what she does. But can she now? When she most needs to? Can she do it and hold it under pressure?

She stares at me for a moment. Too long before giving a less-than-convincing nod. She takes a deep breath and her body shimmers before my eyes, the neutral tone of her draki flesh dimming until it appears as if she's gone, vanished.

I still feel her beside me, clutching my arm. I stare down at the hunters far below. Several wear a contraption on their faces that resembles heavy goggles. I narrow my gaze, wondering at this device, when it dawns on me. I've seen my share of spy movies.

'No,' I whisper.

Infrared goggles. Considering they detect body heat, I must be glowing like a bonfire in our hiding spot. Miram won't be safe either, even invisible.

Miram tenses beside me. 'What?'

I don't have time to explain. A hunter shouts, pointing, 'There! In that tree!'

A launcher pops and a net hisses as it flies through the air. I'm hit. *We're* hit—since Miram hasn't left my side.

There are too many branches. The net can't close around us properly. Instead it tangles us hopelessly together, stopping us from simply flying away. Miram freaks, flapping her wings fiercely, making it harder to fight free of the rope mesh.

She thrashes like a caught bird, whimpers like a wild animal. Faint color flashes, bursts of pale light, there one moment and gone the next.

'Get a grip,' I growl, 'you're . . . materializing . . . they can see you.'

Below us, they shout instructions at each other, strategizing, doing what they do best. What they've trained their whole lives to do. Hunt draki. There's no time. They'll have us down from this tree in a matter of seconds.

Instinct kicks in. Char and ash fill my mouth. Smoke shivers from my nostrils, puffs from my lips. The smolder rides high in my chest, hungry to defend and protect.

I part my lips and blow a thin ribbon of flame, just enough to burn through the mesh tangled near my face. Just enough for me to grasp the hot, seared edges and tear a hole large enough to squeeze through.

With half my body free, I turn back to haul a mostly invisible Miram out after me. She's still flashing in and out, a light blinking on and off.

That's when I'm hit. A harpoon grazes my thigh. Pain lances my body. I slap a hand over the torn, wet flesh.

Over their rapid-fire shouts, I fall. Just like in my nightmares. I'm plunging toward the ground. Tangled net and Miram, too.

We land in a winded, broken pile. My lungs heave, contracting with heat, the air around me thin and brittle, ice compared to the intense warmth frothing inside me.

Instantly, they surround us. Black-clad figures with their infrared goggles. Weapons point. They shout in their hard voices. And I see a face. One that I could never forget no matter how much I might want to block it from my memory.

Staring up into Xander's relentless face, I know who these hunters are. As if there were ever a doubt. I know Will can't be very far. Except this doesn't fill me with relief. It's closer to despair.

What can Will do? He can't do anything to help me without risking himself, without exposing that I'm more than I appear.

Still, I search—long for a glimpse of him—as I shouldn't.

More vehicles arrive, screeching to a halt, spraying dirt into the thick mist.

Miram speaks feverishly in my ear, her panic palpable, a hot wind I can taste, bitter and acrid on the air. 'Jacinda, Jacinda! What do we do? What do we do?'

'Shut up, Miram,' I hiss, the draki-speech thick in my mouth.

The choppers circle like dark vultures, whipping the trees into a frenzy all around us. My hair blows wildly amid flying leaves.

One of the hunters rips off his goggles for a better look at me. He inches closer and prods me with the sharp tip of his gun. A growl swells up from my too-tight chest, dark and menacing. A sound I did not even know I was capable of. He prods at Miram's blurring form beside me. 'What in the hell . . .' His voice fades as another hunter barks at him.

'Carl, back off. We don't know what we have here yet.'

The hunter obeys, edging back from us.

'Miram,' I plead, 'stay invisible. Focus.'

Her eyes hold mine, the vertical pupils shuddering, vanishing and reappearing with the rest of her. She's like rippling water, seemingly amorphous, constantly altering, there and then gone again.

Bodies clamber from the vehicles. I tear my attention back to these men with their merciless faces, search among them, looking for a chance, a hope.

Will's not among them. Even as relief runs through me, I can't help wondering why. *Why* isn't he here? Where is he?

I recognize the man striding at the front of the group. Will's father. Still handsome and well-groomed even in his hunting apparel. A hot trickle of terror shivers up from my core. Because I know what this man is capable of.

He looks different. Not the cordial man who welcomed me into his home when he thought I was a normal girl. His brutally cold eyes assess me, see me as a creature. Prey. And I see him. Truly see him. He'll have no problem snuffing out my life.

'What do we have here, boys?'

'We've got two . . . well, we think.'

Mr Rutledge stares hard at us for a moment. Miram's out of control next to me, and I know it's useless to tell her to hold it together anymore. She's too afraid. Too panicked.

I scan the thick press of trees, each beat of my heart a loud, reverberating thump in my chest. My razor-sharp gaze skips over each hunter, hungry for the sight of one face. Against all sanity, I still hope. *Will, where are you?*

Xander steps close to his uncle and motions to Miram. 'That's one of those invisible ones.' He points at me. 'Know what type that one is?'

Mr Rutledge studies me without answering, his head angled as though he can dissect me with his eyes. And I suppose he can. I have trouble meeting his gaze—this man who is Will's father, who butchered my kind and infused their lives' blood into his son. For that he is a monster. *But for that his son lives, a boy I love.*

It's a twisted reality, and I can't help hearing Cassian in my head, insisting that someday that very thing would drive a wedge between Will and me.

Mr Rutledge stretches out a hand and flicks his fingers, apparently reaching a decision. Instantly, a weapon appears, placed in his hand. A gun of some kind. I know nothing about them except that they hurt. They destroy.

He aims.

Miram thrashes wildly, watching in horror as I do.

Only I cannot simply *watch*. Not when the core of me is a weapon.

Hot purpose rolls over me. 'Stop,' I snarl, for all they can't understand me, shoving Miram away from me so that I can do what needs to be done. What I'm born to do. But we're tangled in the net, and she won't stop clinging to me, pleading in low rumbling draki-speech.

Shaking hair from my face, I part my lips and blow.

Fire fights its way up my throat. My windpipe shudders with raging heat. The steam releases from my nostrils an instant before flames burst from my lips. With a roar the blast of heat arcs across the air. The hunters cry out, dance back from the far-reaching flames.

The net falls from us, incinerated to tufts of ash. The taste of char and cinder coats my mouth. I grab Miram's arm and haul her up off the ground. She's uncooperative, dead weight in her fear.

My face tilts to the sky, eager for escape, freedom, hungry for wind, but not without her. 'Get up!' I cry. 'C'mon! Fly!'

She starts to rise, her movements sluggish. With all my strength, I lift her up, ready to ascend even if it means carrying her.

My feet leave the ground just as I'm hit. Pain erupts in my wing, misery that lances through the membrane. They're deceptive: draki wings look gossamer soft, but are really quite strong, laced with countless nerves that make them all the more sensitive. *I'm in agony.*

Twisting my body up into the air, I tear the small harpoon from my wing, fling it until it impales in the soft ground.

I collapse back down, head bowed in pain.

Miram breaks from my side, stumbles, lost from me in our fall.

Will's dad steps closer, his weapon aimed at me. His eyes are cold. He feels nothing.

There's a whistle as I'm hit again. In the thigh. This time the pain is less, not another harpoon. My gaze jerks down, rests on the dart protruding from my red-gold flesh. I yank it free and glare at it, see that it contains a vial. A now-empty vial.

A second whistle cuts the air. My gaze swerves, watches as the dart hits with a solid *thunk* into Miram's body. She screams. The sound is bewildered, stunned only as one who's never endured physical pain before can feel.

And yet I know it's more than the pain. It's the fear, this horror of being treated like an animal without worth. Something to be hunted, caught, and ultimately destroyed.

I drag myself to her side. She slumps against me, her tears moist on my shoulder, a chilling hiss on my scalding flesh.

I shout at the hunters even though I know that I probably appear more animal to them with my strange, growling sounds. More the beast that needs exterminating. I cringe, wither inside at the sensation of their cold, apathetic eyes on me.

In moments, my vision grows fuzzy. My head feels warm, insulated. And somehow I don't care anymore. I feel good all over, tingly.

The hunters descend, smudges of dancing black. A roaring fills my ears, but not loud enough to cover Miram's gasping sobs. Those I hear. Those I will always hear.

I squeeze her hand, or at least I try to. My muscles are so tired, feeble and sluggish. I'm not sure I do anything more than cover her fingers with mine. Then, she's no longer with me. They take her, drag her from my side. I stretch for her, but I'm too slow. Her talons claw through the earth, leave deep gouges in the soil. Her screams don't sound so close anymore, but they're still there, fading in the distance like a dying wind.

'Where are you taking her?' I shout in my guttural tongue. 'Miram! Miram!'

Then they come at me with their groping hands.

'Careful *that* one doesn't burn you,' one of the hunters advises.

Blurry figures surround me, I fight the drugging sensation that makes me want to curl into a small ball with a smile on my face and sleep.

I rise up to my knees in a final attempt to escape . . . to get away, flutter my wings and take to the skies. I cry out and fall back down, face-first in the loamy earth. Useless. Raw pain fires through the membrane of my wing, deep into my muscles.

Warm blood flows, gliding down my back, and pooling at the base of my spine. I feel its trickle. Smell the richness.

I drop my head. My hair falls in a fiery curtain around me. And I see it. See the telltale shimmer of my blood, a lustrous purple dripping like spilled ink to the ground.

Still, I fight the numbing lethargy threatening to swallow me. My arms shake trying to lift myself back up. My body is so heavy. Lead.

What was in that vial?

Desperate fury pounds through me, blistering along my veins. I want to unleash myself, burn them all, punish them for what they're doing to me—and all they plan to do. Things so terrible we've never been directly told. No one sits us down in primary school and explains what really happens once a hunter captures us and turns us over to the enkros, but I know. I saw Will's father's study—the furniture covered in draki skin.

I open my mouth and release another gust of fire—my last hope. A thin thread of flame spills past my lips. This time the fiery breath withers almost the moment it's released, dies in a trail of steam.

'Will,' I croak, my eyelids heavy, impossible to hold up anymore.

Hard hands grip me on all sides, lifting me up. I turn my face and try to blow flame on the arms, but only choke out a weak rivulet of steam.

What did they do to me?

They bind my hands, my wrists squeezed so tightly blood ceases to flow. Even groggy, I feel this new pain. I'm flipped on my stomach, straddled. Again, I'm just an animal, a beast. A scream rises in my throat as my wings are bound tight to each other, preventing them from moving, preventing me from flight.

I'm tossed through the air, striking hard, smooth ground. The surface is cold and frigid against my hot flesh. Not dirt then.

Doors slam. I'm in the back of a vehicle. A van. It begins moving, bumping over the ground, weaving through trees and clawing foliage. Taking me farther from the pride. Farther from home.

I can't fight anymore. My lids sink over tired eyes. Even with my body's discomfort, with the sting pulsing in my wing, vibrating deep into my shoulder blades, I can't resist the drug's soporific effect. My cheek presses down on the cold metal floor and I slip into sleep.

18

Pain greets me when I wake.

I take several slow blinks before I manage to fully open my eyes. The torment in my head rivals the intense throbbing everywhere else in my beaten and broken body and I have to close my eyes again for several moments before opening them again.

My wings throb. I try to move the gossamer sheets, and the pain jolts deep, radiating along my entire length. I'd forgotten they were strapped together. I curl up into a small ball and moan my misery.

After a while and several deep breaths later, I lift my head, peel my cheek from the cold metal floor of the van. I shake my head, wondering if I'm even awake, wondering if this is all a nightmare.

I catch the sound of a whimper nearby. I turn, spot Miram pressed along a far wall of the van. With great effort I lift up, so glad to see her that for a moment the pain doesn't matter. At least we're together in this metal box.

'Miram,' I whisper, dragging myself closer to her, relieved that she's here.

She's visible, of course. Her eyes lock on mine.

I wet my dry lips. 'What . . .'

'What happened?' Miram finishes my question. 'You,' she says. 'You always happen. I suppose it's not such a surprise this would be your fate, but I can't believe I'm here, too. That you've dragged me into this . . .'

'We're going to get out of this,' I promise. It's all I can say, all I can believe.

'Yeah,' she snarls. The ridges of her nose flex with hot emotion. 'And how are you going to manage that?'

'I've escaped them before.'

'OK.' She nods her head savagely, sandy brown hair tossing wildly around the tan, neutral tone of her draki flesh. 'How? How are we going to do that? How'd you do it last time?'

Will. Will is how I escaped. Except he isn't here. I have to figure a way out of this for myself. For both of us.

Miram fills the silence, her voice eerily flat. 'They're taking us to the enkros. We're as good as dead.'

'You don't know that,' I whisper, testing the plastic ties at my wrists with my teeth. Useless.

'Oh, face it, Jacinda. Where else could we be going? *Alive?* They haven't killed us. Clearly there's a reason for that. They're saving us for something. For . . . them.' *Them*. The monsters of our childhood nightmares. Heat feathers along my flesh.

She's right. I know it of course. That's how hunters live. They flourish through selling my kind. I can't deny this.

'How long was I out?' I ask, turning my attention to our surroundings and focusing on something I can control.

Assessing the situation we're in so that I can come up with a plan.

Except there isn't much to see. Only one small window positioned high in the van's back door. Impossibly small. It only lets light in. Nothing out.

'I don't know. I woke up hours ago.'

'They have to stop eventually,' I say, more to myself than her.

'Yeah, so they stop. Then what? Those doors aren't going to open until we reach wherever it is they're taking us. And at that point . . .' Her voice fades.

I grimace, release a slow breath against the unremitting agony of my bound wings. 'I'm not giving up. I've got fire, and you can make yourself invisible.' If she could focus her talent and not cave in to her fear. 'There's no reason anyone should be able to take us down.'

'And yet they did.' Miram arches a fine eyebrow, as tan and nondescript as the rest of her. The ridges of her nose shiver with angry breath as she glares at me. 'So, genius, how are we getting out of this?'

Will. The thought of him is there again, but I don't say it. Don't dare. Why would I want to plant that hope? Even in myself. I have no idea where he is, why he didn't meet me. For now, I need to rely on me.

I shake my head. Still, I can't stop the longing from creeping in. He has to know. By now—he has to have heard of the fire-breather his father captured.

It's this that keeps me calm as we hurl headlong into the hazy realm of my nightmares, the wind buffeting the van and sending shudders up my body.

* * *

They don't stop for us. Not to feed us or offer us a chance to relieve ourselves. But then why would they afford us such a simple courtesy? We're just animals to them.

The van is hot and suffocating, an airless metal box rumbling along dispassionately.

Miram and I lie on our sides, roasting on the hot metal floor like two parched fish tossed from the sea, desperate to return to water. We've long since stopped speaking to each other, too miserable with our bound hands and hobbled wings.

I can't move without spiking pain through my body. I continually lick my cracked lips, swallow against the misery of my dry mouth. Breathing fire seriously depleted me. My insides are shriveling up, desperate for water.

But I haven't quit. I'm reserving my strength, waiting for the van doors to open so that I might burst free in a blaze of fire.

I *tell* myself this. Believing I can summon enough fire is harder to do.

I no longer feel my wings. I try not to think about that, about what that might mean. It can't be good. Lying on my side, my arms pressed close to my chest, they burn, tingle with pinpricks of pain.

The van slows. I slide a bit as the vehicle turns.

We stop. I can't even summon much excitement. We've already stopped before. No one opened the door to check on us. They just gassed up, did whatever they had to do for themselves, and left us roasting in the back.

It doesn't mean the doors will open now. Still . . .

I lift my head and whisper Miram's name, just to make sure she's awake. The sound comes out a croak. She doesn't respond. Doesn't move. I drag myself closer and nudge one of her sleek legs with my foot. 'Miram!'

She moans and cracks her eyes open. 'What?'

'We've stopped.'

'So?' she rasps.

I cock my head, listening as the driver and passenger doors slam open and shut. Voices. The words are indecipherable.

She struggles to a sitting position, pushing up, using her bound arms for leverage. 'Think we're here?' She asks this so listlessly that I'm not sure she would even care if that were the case.

I shake my head, my every agonized muscle braced, pulled tight, thrumming in readiness. My ears strain, following the sound of their tread, the crunch of gravel beneath their feet as they circle the van. One laughs, the sound fading as they walk away, leave the van. Leave *us*.

After a moment I release my breath, unaware that I had been holding it. 'They're gone,' I whisper, then, realizing there's no need, I repeat louder, 'They're gone.'

'Probably to feed their fat faces,' she mutters. 'I would kill for something to eat.'

With a sigh, she settles back down on the van floor. I look at her. Really look at her. Always small, she appears emaciated, her face gaunt, her breath raspy. Her chest lifts high, laboring for each breath. Maybe my time in the desert prepared me for this. Arid heat. Discomfort. Misery. Because Miram isn't holding up well, and she didn't even take a harpoon to the wing.

160

I have to get her out of here. Soon. Or these hunters will be arriving at their destination with one dead draki.

Suddenly there's a sharp sound at the door. I spring to a crouch, a surge of adrenaline staving off the pain. Something scrapes against the metal door. The scratch of metal raises the tiny hairs on my nape. My gaze drills into the doors. I inhale, readying myself, letting heat build and gather at my core.

Weak and parched as I am, the effort nauseates me, leaves me shaking and wasted. I'm not at full strength, but it has to be enough. I'll get only one chance. I have to be ready for whoever opens that door.

'Miram,' I say, wishing she could get it together and make herself invisible—and hold it. 'Get ready.'

She gives a small nod.

Curling steam wafts from my nose.

I part my lips, staring so hard at the door my eyes start to ache. There's a thud followed by a sucking sound as the door pulls open. My heart clenches in my smoldering chest. Midday light pours inside the van in liquid-hot rays, momentarily blinding me. I don't care though—can't hesitate and lose my chance.

I reach deep, find smoldering heat where I feared none was left. Fire heats my windpipe, bursts free in a gust of flame. It's enough.

The figure outlined in the afternoon light dives to the ground with a cry.

I jump from the van and manage to keep my balance on unsteady legs—especially hard to do with my hands and wings bound.

I bend down to search the hunter's pockets for a weapon, something to cut into the binding on my wrists. And I freeze.

It's not one of the several hard-eyed, black-clad hunters who trussed me up like a holiday goose and tossed me into the back of a van. It's Will.

A sharp, strangled sound rises from the back of my throat. I choke his name, a sound he can't possibly comprehend.

But he doesn't need to understand. He knows. He's here for me. That's all that matters. And that I didn't incinerate him.

He's on his feet, sliding his hands up my trembling arms as if verifying that I'm real, that I'm before him. 'Jacinda!'

Relief rushes over me. My adrenaline takes a dive, and the pain and weariness flood back, closing me in a clenching, unrelenting fist. I give in, collapse in his arms—let him rescue me, save me from his kind, from the agony that screams through every particle of my being.

Will carefully wraps an arm around me, looking over my shoulder at my strapped wings. I feel his wince as he takes measure.

Anxiety radiates from him, underlies his movements as he handles me, trying to guide me away from the van. His changeable eyes dart, scan the mostly vacant truck-stop parking lot.

I hold back, peer inside the van. 'Miram,' I say, the urgency sharp in my voice. 'Let's go.'

She hovers in the far shadows, where the sunlight doesn't reach, fiercely shaking her head side to side.

'Miram!' I repeat her name, sounding like a parent addressing a child that refuses to obey.

She shakes her head harder, her eyes fixed on Will. 'I won't go with *him*.'

'Don't be stupid. He's here to help us—'

'What if it's a trap? What if he's just tricking you into going along meekly, like a lamb to the slaughter?'

'Do you even know how ridiculous you sound? Why would they do that? We're already their prisoners.' I move between the van's open doors, beseeching her with my eyes. Still, she shakes her head, shrinks back against the far wall as if *I* were the threat. 'You'll risk remaining in this van rather than going with us?'

Will tugs on my arm. 'Jacinda! They'll be back any second. This is our only chance!'

'Miram, please,' I beg. 'Trust me.'

She jerks her chin once at Will. 'I don't trust him.' Then her eyes fix steadily on me. 'Or you.'

Anger sparks my blood. *She* doesn't trust *me*. She's the one who's been spying on me!

Will's voice falls hard near my ear. His fingers flex on my arm, no longer so gentle. 'Jacinda, they're coming!'

I go. Tearing myself away, I leave her.

But not without her wide, haunted eyes imprinted on my soul.

19

Will drags me across the parking lot. It's an odd sensation. Running in broad daylight in full manifest in the human world. Such a strange, forbidden thing. Anyone could see me.

Not that I have a choice.

It's either stay in the van, a prisoner awaiting execution, or risk the fifteen-second dash to the shelter of the waiting woods. For me, it's an obvious choice. Why couldn't Miram see that, too?

Will and I dive into the thick growth of trees edging the parking lot. One moment cracked asphalt burns beneath my feet, the next it's the yielding, whispering soil of the forest floor.

A sense of desolation rises up inside me, suffocating. I look over my shoulder as if I can see the van through the press of foliage.

I've left Miram. I've failed her. *Failed Cassian.*

I blink stinging eyes and tell myself it's the sudden sunlight. The sweeping, incomprehensible pain hammering my body. Not this invading sorrow for the girl I left behind and what will become of her.

Will's Land Rover isn't far. He helps me inside. I prop myself on the passenger seat, mindful to sit forward. It's impossible to lean back with my wings bound tight.

There's a flash of light in Will's hand and I realize he's holding a knife. He swipes through my wrist ties and I sigh. Except the relief is brief, eclipsed as feeling rushes back into my hands in a searing flood of agony. I moan. Drop my head.

Will hands me a bottle of water and moves to check my back, his fingers gentle on my bare shoulders. I drink deep, noisily, water running down my chin and throat.

Over my gulps, I hear his sharp intake of breath as he saws through the bindings. 'You're hurt.' A curse follows this, humming with an anger I've never heard from him. And something else. *Regret? Guilt?*

'They shot my wing.' The words rumble from my throat. At the guttural sound, I remember he can't understand me.

He's quiet for a moment, and then he says quickly, as if remembering the danger encroaching all around us, 'It doesn't look too bad.' His voice is a low rasp and I know he's lying. It looks bad.

With a final jerk of his hand, my wings spill free. Again, agony. Red-hot as fresh blood rushes back into the abused appendages. The sensation makes the edges of my vision gray, my head spin. I open my mouth wide on a silent scream.

This pain is worse than the last time I was hit, the first time hunters pursued me. The pain was intense then, but I healed. Mom treated the wound . . . *Mom*. Has she left her room? Did she even notice I was gone? The notes won't be waiting for her.

Will's anxious eyes flit over me, and then to the surrounding press of trees. 'We've got to go . . . Jacinda, can you change?'

He's asking if I can demanifest.

I nod once. The fear is gone—can't force me to stay a draki any longer. At the moment there is only pain . . . and more pain to come as I force my wings to merge back inside me. Especially the injured wing. But there is no choice. He can't drive out of here with me sitting in the front seat in full manifest.

I take a deep gulp and clench the edge of the seat with bloody-slick fingers, burying my draki, pushing it back down, hiding it away.

My features relax and loosen, bones decompressing. My wings shudder, quake from their recent abuse. One wing settles back between my shoulder blades with ease. The other one possesses a life of its own, quivering, resisting the demanifest . . . the pain. Tears stream down my cheeks in steaming paths. I arch my neck, fight the scream that bubbles there.

With my draki finally buried, I breathe again, ease my grip on the dash, and crumple back against the seat.

Will tosses a blanket over me. Even though I was trapped in a hot, airless van for a day, I snuggle into the scratchy fabric, glad for the comfort.

'Jacinda, are you OK?'

I try to still the trembling aftershocks, but the harder I resist, the more fiercely the shudders rack me. 'Just get me out of here.' The words sound rusty, unnatural.

With a single nod, he's around the truck and inside the car in a flash. Soon, he's guiding the vehicle out of the woods, through the thick trees until he reaches a small country road leading somewhere. Anywhere. Away. Nothing else really matters but that.

I slide weakly in the seat, reach out a hand, and brush the sun-warmed glass of the window. The pads of my fingers squeak as they slide against the smooth surface. *Miram.*

'Where were you?' I manage to choke out in a scratchy voice.

'I couldn't come. Out of nowhere, Dad scheduled a hunt. Ever since we spotted you, he's obsessed over that same area. He paired me up with a group that he sent out on the other side of the mountain. I hoped if I didn't show up you would just head back home. I didn't think they would move so close to the pride. God, Jacinda, I'm so sorry.'

I nod numbly. 'You didn't know.'

He releases a heavy breath and I know my words do nothing to alleviate his guilt. If I could say more to make him feel better, I would. I just hurt too much.

I lift my legs up on the seat and hug my knees, thinking about the girl I left behind. Thinking about Cassian's face when he finds out.

'You couldn't have helped her,' Will says, reading my thoughts. 'She wouldn't leave.'

'I should have forced her.'

'And caused a scene? You could hardly walk yourself. I practically had to carry you.'

This doesn't comfort me. I lift my head, relishing the cool breeze of air-conditioning on my face.

'Rest now, Jacinda. You're safe.'

Safe. The word trips through my mind until I feel so dizzy I have to close my eyes. My lids sink, so incredibly heavy. Bursts of color flash against the solid black, but it's still better than opening my eyes again and facing the world.

Somewhere between thoughts of Miram and safety and the pain plaguing my body, I surrender to sleep.

I wake in a mostly darkened room. A dull orange light hugs one wall. I sit up, wincing at the pull in my back. With the pain comes reality.

'Will?'

'I'm right here.'

I follow the sound of his disembodied voice and locate him. His dark shape unfolds from a chair in the corner.

'Where are we?'

'In a motel. We're safe.'

I carefully maneuver myself into a sitting position, biting my lips against the ache of my tender back. Still, it's nothing compared to before. I can at least move without feeling the overwhelming need to scream. 'How'd we get here?'

'You were exhausted. You needed rest. On an actual bed. Food, water—'

At the mention of food, my stomach growls.

'I got you to eat a little before you passed out,' he adds. 'Do you remember? You consumed a burrito and soda in less than a minute before dropping into bed. You haven't moved from that spot. Not even when I cleaned and bandaged your back. I was so worried.'

I shake my head. 'I can't remember any of that.'

'You've been through a lot.'

I nod. Sleep must have been my body's way to heal. 'How long have I been asleep?'

'Eight, ten hours.'

My entire body tenses. 'Ten hours! What time is it?'

'About one in the morning.'

A thick lump rises in my throat. Miram must be far away by now. She didn't have the luxury of a bed or food. I swing my legs over the bed, my head full of thoughts of reaching her. Saving her. *How could I have left her?*

'Whoa there.' Will sits beside me on the bed, his warm hand on my shoulder. It's a touch I remember. A touch I want to lean into, absorb and forget everything else. 'Where are you going?'

'To get Miram.' Where else? A chill skates over my bare legs as the sheet slips to the side. I glance down and see that I'm wearing only a white undershirt that must belong to Will.

'I helped you into that,' he explains, a faint tinge of red coloring his face.

'Thanks,' I murmur, remembering I didn't have much on when I fell asleep in the passenger seat. Just that scratchy blanket. I curl my fingers around the shirt's hem, feeling suddenly self-conscious. Here I am. Alone in a motel room with Will, but this solitude is not something I can enjoy. Not with everything that has happened.

'Miram's your friend?' he asks quietly, patiently.

I wince. 'Sorta.'

He stares at me starkly, moments stretching between us. 'I'm sorry. Jacinda, she's gone. There's no helping her now.'

'*No!*' I shake my head wildly, a snarl of hair catching in my mouth. I swipe it free. 'It's my fault she was out there—'

'How is it your fault when she wouldn't come with us? There was nothing you could do.'

I ignore his logic, thinking only of Cassian when he learns his sister is lost. 'You can do something! You're one of them—'

He flinches, but I don't care. For once this doesn't twist my stomach into knots. Guilt doesn't ribbon its way through me because I'm in love with one of the monsters that would hunt me, toss me in the back of a van, bind my hands and wings, and then sell me for parts. In this situation, what he is should be a help.

'No, Jacinda. It's done. She's already been delivered . . .'

Delivered. Like she's goods, an inanimate object. A package. I feel something inside me withering, pulling away from him.

'You *won't* help me, you mean,' I announce, my words a hard bite.

The air-conditioning unit near the wide, curtained window kicks to life, a loud rumble in the tiny room. A rush of cool air wafts over me, but even this fails to relieve my skin or calm my nerves.

In the gloom, his features look drawn and tight, pained that he can't—*won't*—give me the words I desperately need to hear. 'I can't,' he repeats. 'She's at the stronghold by now. Nothing escapes that place.'

Nothing escapes that place. Meaning draki captives live there? As prisoners? They don't kill them right away?

A flash of my father intrudes. He slips into my crowded mind. The image of his laughing eyes, his handsome face that I can't recall as clearly anymore, fills my head. Lying in bed late at night, I sometimes flip on the lights and reach for a photograph of him, something real, something I can hold in my hands. Proof that he did exist, that I remember him and see him still, that I will never forget all the wonderful things he taught me. That I never forget him. Never forget his love.

I have no trouble seeing his face now, but I shove the memory aside, not daring to let myself hope for something as unlikely—as impossible—as my father alive after all these years.

'But Miram's alive? They won't have killed her, that's what you're saying.' I stare deeply into his eyes, their color lost to me in the shadowed room.

He winces, like he regrets implying that. 'Yeah,' he admits with a heavy sigh. 'She'll live. If you could call it that. I don't think they've seen too many draki who can make themselves invisible. Just a few. They'll run tests on her . . . take samples. She'll live. For a while, anyway.'

A sick feeling swells up from my stomach, but with it mingles relief. I deliberately keep myself from wondering what they would have done with me. I know from Will that they don't even believe fire-breathers exist anymore. Now they know we do. I do.

What he's telling me about the enkros is more than I've even known, and it gives me hope for Miram.

'So there's a chance—' He starts to shake his head, but I cut him off. 'There's a chance.' I look at him intently. 'With your help, there's a chance.' My hand reaches across the inches separating us and seizes his.

'But there's not. There's no chance.' His voice is deep, that velvet rumble from my dreams pleading with me to accept, to let Miram go.

I can't. I see Cassian's face, my mother's, my sister's . . . the three of them when they're left wondering what happened to us. My heart clutches with a pain that makes all I've endured seem such a small thing. Miram is lost.

Because of me. I can't just run away with Will pretending that didn't happen.

Something in me dies, unravels like the last bit of a frayed rope that can bear no more. My grip loosens on his hand, fingers sliding free. I pull away.

He snatches my hand back, lacing his strong fingers with mine, pressing our palms together in a kiss. 'Jacinda,' he whispers.

I lock eyes with him, see the need there, read the silent question that he's asking me. Know that he wants assurance that we're still on target with our plan.

A part of me longs to give him the assurance he wants. It would be so easy. We're here. Together. I'm already free of the pride. *Free . . .*

But am I? Am I really?

I know the answer in my bones, deep in my gut. Even if it doesn't match up with what my heart feels. Except the way he stares at me just now . . . I can't say the words.

'I-I'm going to take a shower,' I say hastily. 'And then go back to bed. I-I'm still tired.' Not a lie. I feel like I could sleep another ten hours.

For a second I think he's going to push, demand we have this conversation now. And I can't. Not now. I can't tell him there's no way I can run away with him.

How can I be with him? How can I ever feel free if I subject Mom and Tamra to the torment all over again? Just like with Dad. The wondering, the never knowing for sure. The waiting, enduring the passing of days until you finally have to admit that he's gone and never coming back. I can't do that to them again. And there's Miram. I have a responsibility to her family, too.

After a moment, he says, 'I have some clothes you can wear. Another shirt. Some sweats, too.'

I nod, relieved that he's going to let the subject drop. For now.

He stands and I watch as he riffles through his duffel bag and comes out with the clothing. I take the bundle, both thankful and regretful when our hands don't touch this time.

Moving out from his shadow, I step into the light of the bathroom, closing the door on him with a soft click.

20

After a shower, I curl up on the bed, lifting my hair from where it's trapped beneath me and dropping it over my shoulder. For a long time, I hold myself still, silent beneath the sheets as I do my best to ignore Will next to me. I wait for sleep, for the moment when my dizzy, frantic thoughts can slide into rest.

Despite having slept so much already, I'm still tired. My beaten body should be able to fall back asleep. It *should*.

'How long are you going to pretend to be asleep?'

And there's why it can't.

His hushed voice brushes the back of my neck and my flesh puckers to gooseflesh.

He's why I can't sleep. I've been doing my best to block him out. Impossible, of course. How am I supposed to ignore that Will is inches away? Will, who I've longed for since the moment he spared my life months ago in that cave . . . before I even understood that it was longing I felt.

I open my mouth, but then realize speaking only confirms that I'm awake. I seal my lips shut. Because I can't speak. Not when I can't say what he wants to hear.

What even *I* wish I could say.

His hand closes on my shoulder, and a sigh escapes me. So much for faking sleep.

I don't resist as he rolls me over. We sink toward the center of the bed, practically chest to chest. His eyes glow in the dark. His hand moves, lifts.

My breath locks in my lungs as he slides his hand through the snarls of my damp hair, holding me, his face so close that our noses brush. The scent of the motel's complimentary raspberry shampoo swirls around us.

Staring at each other, we don't speak. I taste his breath then, his lips so near my own. When his eyes dip toward my mouth my stomach twists. Familiar heat swamps me. I bite my lip to keep any sound escaping.

And then I can only think that this is Will.

Will who I've wished for and thought lost to me. Will who I've dreamed of. Will who has saved me time and again, who *I* saved at great risk. Who loves me when there is every reason he shouldn't. Who I love despite all the reasons I shouldn't.

Will who I have to leave. Again.

I lift my hands to his chest. Flattening my palms, I try not to caress him, try to find the strength to push him away. It's going to be hard enough saying goodbye tomorrow.

But then he kisses me, and I know I can't pull away.

His hand at the back of my head slides to my face, his warm palm a rasp on my cheek as he swallows up my moan.

The kiss still feels new. Like the first time. The brush of his mouth sends ripples of sensation along every nerve. I clutch his shoulders, clinging, fingers curling into the lean muscles of his body. I hold on for dear life, the mere texture and taste of his mouth completely devastating me.

My body burns, skin pulling and rippling, overcome, ready to fade out.

Maybe it's where we are, the circumstances of what has brought us here . . . or the fact that I may never see him again, but I can't get enough of him. My mouth moves over his, nibbling, sucking.

His hands roam down my back, tugging me closer.

I move in, wind my arms around his neck. Tangling fingers through his hair, I deepen the kiss, not even minding when his full weight rolls hard over me, sinking me deeper into the mattress.

My body cradles his, instinctively welcoming him. I breathe a greedy sound, not even thinking that we might be moving too far, too fast. There's only need. Hunger. I'm tired of being denied.

He grips my head in both hands, kissing me thoroughly, biting at my lips in little nips. His fingers press into the tender flesh of my cheeks, holding my face still for him.

Growling, I struggle to move my head, to taste him as he tastes me, but he holds me, traps me . . . a delicious torment that makes me writhe beneath him.

It isn't enough. Not even close.

Fire froths at my core, and I struggle to rein it in, to cool my lungs.

I whimper when he glides a hand beneath my shirt, caressing my back in sweeping strokes. He lifts his lips from mine to say, 'Your skin . . . so . . . hot.'

176

I gasp sharply against our fused mouths as his hand drifts, brushes my ribs, the quivering skin of my stomach.

I tear my lips free and arch my face away from him to release a steaming breath that I can't hold in any longer.

He drags an icy kiss down my curved throat, his tongue tracing the tendon there . . . only escalating the smolder within me.

His mouth lifts from my neck. Cool air caresses the wet flesh. I gulp the chilly air, desperate to douse the inferno building in me.

I feel his stare. Look up and plunge directly into it.

Even in the room's gloom, his eyes gleam. He stares down at me with such raw intensity that I lift a trembling hand to trace the shadowed outline of his face, caress the hard-etched lines and masculine angles with my fingertips. I brush the dark eyebrows above those eyes that see right through me.

My fingers drift, relax on his mouth, slightly swollen from kissing. His lips move beneath my touch. 'Come with me, Jacinda.' The words rumble through my fingers, up my arm, rooting into my heart. And I go cold.

Because he knows. He knows what's going on in my head. When I escaped into the bathroom tonight, he heard what I wasn't saying, the words I didn't want to speak aloud.

I can't go with him. I can't run away and be with him in this perfect fantasy we've created in our minds.

'I can't,' I whisper. Then louder, 'I can't.'

I push his shoulder until he rolls off me. Even in the dim room, I can see the change in his expression. He looks angry, his expression like granite.

'How can you go back there?'

'I can't *not* go back. They have to know about Miram . . . and I can't leave Mom and Tamra wondering what happened to me.'

'We can send a letter,' he growls.

'This isn't a joke,' I snap.

'Do you see me laughing?' Seizing both my hands, he leans his face close to mine. 'Why are you fighting this? Us?'

I shake my head. 'I can't just leave with things like this.'

'You may never get out again. Have you thought about that?' His hands tighten on mine. 'What are they going to do to you when you waltz in there and tell them you got yourself caught by hunters? That Miram is lost?'

I shiver. He's right. It could get ugly. But not totally undeserved on my part. My selfish desires led to this, after all. If I'd listened to Cassian and ended it with Will none of this would ever have happened.

Of course, Miram played her part, too. I'm not above holding her responsible for her involvement. She shouldn't have been spying on me. That said, she doesn't deserve the fate awaiting her just because she's a nosy, spiteful girl.

'I'm going back.'

'Even if it means we're never together again?'

He knows just what to say. The words that will hurt me the most. The prospect of never seeing him again, hearing his voice, holding him . . .

I wet my lips, swallow, and say words I never thought possible. Words that echo what's in my head if not my heart. 'But we don't really belong together, Will.'

He pulls back, drops my hands like I'm something he can't bear to touch anymore. 'You don't mean that.'

I nod a single time, the motion painful, all I can manage. 'It's insanity. What we are . . .' *What we aren't.* 'You can't deny—'

He flings himself off the bed in an angry move. 'You know the difference between you and me, Jacinda?' he bites out, his voice unfamiliar to me and a little scary.

I scramble into a sitting position, blinking at this angry, unknown Will.

'The difference is that I know who I am.'

I bristle. 'I know who I am!'

'No. You know *what* you are. You haven't figured out *who* you are.'

'I'm someone with sense enough to realize I can't live happily ever after with a hunter—someone with the blood of slaughtered draki running through his veins!' I slap a hand over my mouth the moment this flies from my lips.

He stops, stares down at me with a frightening stillness.

Terrible doesn't describe how I feel in that moment. I told him his blood didn't matter to me, and I meant it. He can't help what he is, so it's vastly unfair to fling that in his face. Without draki blood, he'd likely be dead, and I certainly don't wish that had happened. And he'd been just a kid at the time. A sick, dying kid. It wasn't like he had any choice in his method of treatment. How could I fling that in his face?

'That's it, isn't it? What's really bugging you.'

I shake my head, blink against the sting in my eyes.

He continues, 'You think hooking up with some draki prince, with *Cassian*, makes sense?'

I breathe thinly though my nose. 'Maybe,' I whisper, not even sure what I'm saying. Even if Cassian did make sense, he isn't for me. I'd never betray Tamra that way.

179

He nods, speaks in such a deadened voice that I feel cold inside. 'It would be easy to just accept him. I can understand that.' He motions between us. 'Easier than this . . . us.' He steps closer. His legs brush the mattress. His hand lowers to touch my face then, his fingers feather soft on my cheek. I resist leaning into that hand, resist surrendering to the pull he has over me. 'Only you'll never love him. Not like you love me. Right or wrong, that's the truth. The way it will always be.'

But it can't be. I can't let it.

With a shuddery breath, I turn my face from his hand and glance at the digital clock on the bedside table. 'I'm not going to fall back asleep now. Why don't we get an early start?'

He laughs. The mirthless sound is low and deep, shivering over my skin. 'Fine. Go home. Run away, Jacinda. But it won't change anything. You won't forget me.'

He's right. But I have to do my best to try.

21

'Stop here,' I announce, glancing at the quiet woods surrounding us, satisfied that we're a safe enough distance from pride grounds. Far enough away that we won't risk Nidia detecting us. At least I hope so.

I rub my sweating hands against the soft fabric of the sweatpants I wear and stare out the dirt-spotted windshield. We've spoken little since leaving the motel.

There's nothing left to say. Still, the silence kills me, twists like a blade in my heart. I hate this, hate that it has to end this way. *Hate that it has to end.*

Will shuts off the engine. I close my eyes and inhale his musky, clean scent, listen to his soft sigh beside me . . . commit these things to memory as they're my last of him.

'I'll be back in a week.'

At this, I turn sharply to stare at him, opening my mouth to protest.

'Don't tell me no,' he says harshly. It's a voice I've never heard him use. With me, at least. He leans forward, clutching the steering wheel as though he would bend it with his bare hands. 'I'll see what I can do about your friend. What I can find out . . .'

For a moment, I can't think who he means. My friend? Then I get it. He means Miram.

'I thought you said it was hopeless.'

His eyes hold mine. In the mid-morning light, I see their color. The golds and browns and greens. 'For you, I would do anything. Especially if it means I'll see you again.'

'Don't risk yourself—'

'What do you think I'm doing here, Jacinda?' His gaze searches mine and I feel stupid. Of course, he's risking himself. I'm not the only one with something to lose. With *everything* to lose. 'I think you're worth it, though.'

His words twist through me, make me feel like a quitter for giving up on us. But then I think of everything—*everyone*—I'm putting at risk. The lives affected if I choose Will right now. And I can't do that. It's not just about me.

'One week,' he repeats, and I mull that over.

This may just be his way of seeing me again, of trying to get more time with me . . . to change my mind, but it may also be Miram's only chance.

I grasp the door handle, yank it down.

'Jacinda?'

At the sound of my name, I look back at him, feel a surge of the familiar longing.

'Noon. One week from today,' I agree.

'I'll be here.' He nods, unsmiling, showing no expression as he holds my gaze hostage. His hand comes to rest over mine on the seat. My skin tingles, heats beneath his palm. I close my eyes in a pained blink, the selfish part of me still longing to go with him.

182

I slide my hand free and step from the Land Rover.

For a moment I stare out at the woods, silent and deep, the crowd of high pines casting a wide shadow. The wind blows, rustling leaves. I feel his gaze on me, but I don't look behind me. It's too tempting. Too hard to keep moving if I do.

With a deep breath, I start running. Sprinting through trees that press on me like familiar friends. Only they don't feel so friendly anymore. They feel like the walls of a prison.

The guard makes me wait at the gate, talking into his radio and speaking in a low voice to someone. Severin, I'm sure. Who else would it be?

I glare at the boy as I stand beneath the ivy-covered arch, waiting . . . like an outsider that may or may not be granted admittance.

I spot Nidia hovering in the open door of her cottage, staring out at me with an unreadable gaze. Even she doesn't come forward to meet me, and I wonder if I've lost her, too.

My sister is nowhere in sight, and I can't help wondering whether she's inside that cottage. Whether she senses I'm here, that I've returned, and just doesn't care. Whether she thinks I abandoned her. The thought makes me feel slightly sick, hollow inside. Especially since she was a large part of why I came back. Tamra and Mom.

Severin arrives, sweeping me with his black gaze, fathomless as dark, endless space.

Several elders accompany him, winded, trying to keep up with his loping strides.

Cassian has no trouble. He's there, too, at his father's

side, his gaze hungry for me, gliding over me as if seeking confirmation that I've actually returned, alive and well.

At least someone looks glad to see me.

Cassian steps forward and grasps my arms. 'Jacinda.'

The breathy sound of my name full of relief and hope and expectation makes me look over my shoulder, wishing I were still with Will, wishing that I didn't carry such tragic news.

His hands slide down my arms to my hands, his fingers threading with mine.

'Where's Miram?' Severin asks the question. The question I've returned home to answer. I glance at him, then back to Cassian. Cassian with his deep, searching gaze. Still hopeful. Ever hopeful. His thumbs move in small circles on the backs of my hands.

In my hesitation, others start to demand the same thing.

Where's Miram? Where's Miram?

'I—' I lick at my dry lips.

'Where's my daughter?' Severin's voice cracks on the air.

I say it then. Spit out the words like a terrible poison I need to purge. 'Hunters took her.'

But the poison doesn't leave me. It's still there, pumping through my blood. The guilt. The awful knowledge that I caused this.

Cassian's thumbs still, stop their roving, but I don't look up. Can't meet his gaze.

I nod, the motion painful. 'It's true.'

His hands loosen on mine, barely touching.

'But *you* managed to escape?' Severin sneers. 'Miraculous.'

184

My eyes burn with pricks of heat.

Cassian's hands fall away altogether now.

My hands lower, fingers twitch, empty at my sides. And I don't know where the sudden pain comes from exactly. That Miram is lost . . . maybe forever? That *I'm* responsible for it?

Or from feeling Cassian slip away from me.

Somehow he's become important to me. Maybe he always has been. Even if I don't know what we are to each other. I know that I care about him. That I can't stand losing him *and* Will.

No longer touching, I look at his face, searching for a sign that he doesn't blame me . . . *hate* me.

Severin moves between us and snatches hold of my arm. His fingers are long and thick, covering almost all of my bicep, and I'm reminded that he's the alpha of our pride for a reason. The largest and strongest draki among us. Someday the alpha will be Cassian, but until then it's Severin. And I'm at his mercy.

He pulls me along and I stifle a wince at his ungentle grasp. I've experienced worse pain over the last few days. Maybe I even deserve this. I just told him his daughter was taken by hunters, after all. I might as well have announced her death.

My feet trip to keep up with him. The others fall behind. I fight the urge to look and see if Cassian follows, too.

'Where are we going?' I dare the question and then regret it when Severin slides me a look of pure loathing. I've never seen such emotion from him. It was never personal before. I was simply a means to an end. A tool for him to use and manipulate.

The town is silent as we cut a line through the mist and head down Main. Hardly any people outdoors. Strange for midday, this lack of activity. It reminds me of the tomblike stillness after my father's disappearance. The pride was in lockdown for more than a month then, no one emerging from their houses. Only the most basic needs were met—the most critical jobs performed for the day-to-day functioning of the pride. I remember some of the other kids complaining that it was the most boring time. I only thought it was the most miserable.

All that floods back now, rushes over me in a bitter tide of memory. I'm there again. Only then I believed in the promise for a better future. That Dad might actually return. Because that's what Mom whispered in our ears, what she would repeat over and over as she put Tamra and me to sleep at night. Now I know the truth. She was either lying to us or to herself because she didn't know any such thing.

Suddenly she's the one I want to see. Like then, I want Mom to comfort me. Hold me and tell me everything is going to be all right. Even if I know better. Even if I can't believe that anymore.

Mom's eyes are dead pools, hardly flickering to life when I enter the house with Severin at my side. The others remain on the porch. Except Cassian. He's gone.

Mom stares at me like she doesn't know me, doesn't see me.

'Mom.' I crouch down beside the bed.

Her glassy-eyed stare flits over my face. She lifts a hand and brushes the tangle of my hair.

'Mom, it's me,' I say. 'I'm back. I'm OK.'

At last her lips move. She murmurs my name. The odor hits me. I glance to the nightstand, spot the bottle of verda wine.

Severin snorts. 'Doubt she even realized you were missing.'

I glance up at his hard face, then look back at Mom. Have I done this? Made things so hard she's drowned herself in a bottle?

Pounding feet rush from outside. Voices carry.

Tamra bursts into the room, Az close on her heels. I rise, my breath a shudder, uncertain what to expect from her, from either of them.

'You're alive,' Tamra chokes.

Her hair isn't its usual tamed perfection. The silvery white mane is as frizzy and wild as my hair. In fact, she looks a complete mess from head to toe. More like me in a pair of shredded jeans and T-shirt.

I nod. 'I'm alive.'

Moments pass and she doesn't move. Doesn't speak as we stare at each other. And then we're in each other's arms. Sobbing.

At first I think the tears are hers, the ugly raw sounds all her. But then I feel the wetness on my cheeks, the vibrations in my throat and chest. I'm crying with her.

Az is there, too, her slim hands stroking my sore back.

'I'm so sorry, Tam,' I say.

'No, I'm sorry! I always blame you for everything and you just put up with it! I'm so glad you're not dead . . . so glad you're back.'

I close my eyes in relief. *This*. This is why I had to come back. Because a part of me will always be linked to Tamra. I couldn't have left her to wonder, to suffer the mystery of my disappearance . . .

'Yes, *she's* alive, but Miram is lost. My *daughter*.' Severin's voice intrudes and we all three peel apart. I stare at him, wary of him as any beast or predator. His attention settles on me. 'This shall not go unpunished. Not this time. You've used up your last chance, Jacinda.'

A creaky floorboard draws my attention to the bedroom door. Cassian stands there, not stepping inside. But he's here. He's come back. Something flutters inside my chest.

'The pride shall assemble within the hour.' My gaze snaps back at the sound of Severin's voice. 'You'll speak for your transgressions so all can hear.'

I'm to face a public judgment?

Such events are uncommon in pride life. I recall only one or two public judgments in my lifetime, but then rarely does anyone transgress.

Severin's dark eyes narrow on me. 'Don't be late. You don't want me to send an escort.' He turns to leave. At the door, he pauses, assesses his son. 'Actually, Cassian. On second thought, why don't you make certain she's on time?'

He means make sure I don't escape.

The relief I felt at the sight of Cassian vanishes. He's to be my jailer.

'It will be OK.' Tamra squeezes my arm, pulling my attention back to her earnest face. 'I'll stand by you.'

'Me too,' Az pipes in.

I smile at the both of them. 'I'm so lucky to have you.'

I glance at Mom. Surprisingly, she's pushing up from the bed. I grasp her arm to help her sit upright.

'I'll make some tea,' Az quickly volunteers, hurrying from the bedroom.

188

Cassian watches in silence from the door as Tamra and I tend to our mother.

'A little privacy please,' Tamra calls sharply at him without looking. Instantly, I'm reminded of the last time the three of us were in a room together. The ugly words . . . Apparently, my sister hasn't forgotten either.

From the corner of my eye, I observe his departure. Listen to his footsteps. He doesn't go far. Just to the living room. He has his orders. He's my escort to the assembly, after all. He won't be leaving.

As though she can read my mind, Tamra says, 'We'll be with you, Jace. Mom and me. We'll stand together as a family.'

I look at my sister as she crouches near Mom. Mom is looking at me, too, her gaze more lucid, more familiar than the stranger's of the last few weeks. More like the mother I know.

'You came back. You voluntarily came back. That has to mean something,' she says, making me feel less worried. And relieved. She knew I'd left. She knew and cared. 'You're no deviant. Severin is not thinking rationally. They'll see that. No one has been punished unjustly before.'

I'm tempted to ask, *What about justly?*

I'm no innocent. I've done things I shouldn't.

But then Mom takes my hand and her grip is warm and firm. Feels the way it did when I was small and she was my entire world. When she and Dad could make everything right with the touch of a hand.

Suddenly, I don't feel so alone. Whatever happens, I know I've got my family. This fortifies me, makes me think I can handle anything.

22

Tamra holds my hand as we walk to the center of town. Others are out, walking in a steady stream in the same direction. They stare openly at me through the sifting curls of mist—even point to me. They don't seem to care that I can see them doing this. And why should they? In their eyes, I'm the one who's done something wrong and been called before the pride to face public judgment.

Tamra gives my hand a reassuring squeeze.

We keep our pace slow enough for Mom. She walks at my other side, squinting at the ribbons of dull light breaking through the mist. Like a mole emerging into day.

When we reach the meeting hall, it's already crowded. The low drone of conversation dies down as I come into view.

Bodies part, peel back, and allow me to walk up the front steps.

Severin stands there behind the stone railing. The half-dozen elders are there, too, puppets behind him. I'm no fool. The *public* will decide nothing. Whatever happens will be his call.

Cassian does not move to stand among them. I guess he can't. Not yet. He has no true official capacity. Instead, he takes a position at the front of the gathered onlookers.

I loosen my fingers to release Tamra's hand and ascend the steps, but she tightens her grip. Doesn't let go.

'I'll go with you,' she says.

Az nods encouragingly behind her. Like she agrees that would be best.

'No. I have to go alone.' I doubt they would let anyone stand up there with me anyway. I look from Tamra to Mom to Az. 'Wait here.' I give a wobbly smile. For them. 'I'll be back. Everything will be fine.' I say this for them, too. I'm not sure what's about to happen. My stomach twists, dips in a sickening lurch. Still, I can't regret returning. I had to. For my family. For Miram and Cassian.

As I stand beside Severin, my infractions are read. He starts with the small.

Neglecting to show up for duty.

Leaving pride grounds without authorization.

I cringe, thinking of the crowd's reaction if they'd known why I had left. *For whom.* That would be yet another infraction. Severin's voice rolls on.

Flight during daylight hours.

Contact with hunters.

His voice bites the air, hard, emotionless. I can't stop the bitter thought from entering my head: of course he won't mention that he's the one who set Miram to spy on me.

'We have these rules for the safety and preservation of our pride. For the protection of our race. When one of us holds herself separate and above the laws of the pride, that draki endangers us all.'

191

I stand with my shoulders back and stare out at the crowd of my brethren. Their expressions are so rapt, so . . . expectant. Something big is about to happen and they know it . . . salivate for it. All of them. I scan the familiar faces, my old friends, neighbors, teachers. Suddenly they seem very *unfamiliar* to me. I long for someone who eases my heart. Someone who has no place here. *Will.*

Severin continues, 'That is precisely what has happened. Miram, my own daughter, is lost to us forever. Even as I stand here, she is at the mercy of the enkros, suffering untold atrocities. Jacinda must pay for her fault in that.'

There is a slight sound in the gathered crowd at this . . . a general murmur I take as assent. I swallow painfully, staring straight ahead, avoiding looking to my family, at Tamra and Mom, at Az . . . Cassian.

I hold myself as tightly as stretched wire and wait for the final verdict, knowing it has come to this. There will be no sparing me. Not this time. Not again. Severin has decided my fate.

I make a sound, a tortured half-laugh. Who am I kidding? His decision was made the moment I returned without Miram.

Still, I jerk at the announcement:

'There is no choice but to clip the wings of any draki whose continued insubordination puts us all at risk.' He motions to me with a sweep of his hand. 'In accordance with ancient tradition, any draki who risks the pride forfeits the gift of flight for however long is necessary.' A hush falls, the silence so deafening I can actually hear the rush of blood to my head.

However long is necessary. Meaning however long it takes my wings to mend. If they ever do. Sometimes damaged or injured wings can't heal properly, leaving a draki permanently crippled.

The air comes alive with a sudden shout from Tamra. Her shrill voice reverberates over the humming silence. 'No! No! You can't do this!' Her face burns with more color than I've seen on her since she manifested. 'It's barbaric! Leave her alone! There is nothing *just* about this!'

Mom's face leaches of all color as she wraps an arm around Tamra, holding her back when she looks ready to charge up the steps. Tamra struggles a moment before burying her face against Mom.

Mom's eyes are no longer dead, no longer empty. But I almost wish they were. Better that than this. So full of anguish and pain.

Severin ignores the outburst, only the slightest tic in his cheek showing he even heard Tamra—or disapproved. It's Tamra. He still needs her, will tolerate her disruption.

His next command slices through me, cutting deep.

'And Zara must bear responsibility as well.' Severin glances to the elders, as if they might object to him dragging my mother into this, before adding, 'Zara is found derelict in her role as a mother and her responsibilities to both child and pride.'

This I did not expect.

'What?' I shout, looking wildly to where my mother stands, her eyes awake, alert and snapping.

Severin continues in a dull monotone. 'She is banished and must leave pride grounds at once. From this day hence, she shall no longer be considered a draki and must make her way in the human world.' Severin's lips curl back from his teeth in a sneer. 'As was always her wish.' He adds this with decided relish, and I know he's enjoying this.

'Wait,' I cry. 'I'll go with her! Banish me, too.'

Severin's lips bend in a slow curl. 'You have no choice in your *punishment*. Besides'—he looks me over coldly, and I feel torn open and bare beneath the thoroughness of his measuring stare—'you will still serve a purpose.'

Curses fly from Tamra's lips. Az clings to her arm, helping restrain her.

I don't know what's worse. The implicit threat that he'll breed me, my imminent wing clipping, or losing Mom. Each is horrible in its separate way.

All will kill a part of me.

This—combined with letting Will and the dream of us go and bearing the guilt of Miram's fate—it's all too much. What else can happen? *What else can I endure?*

I freeze, stilling unnaturally as everything whips past me in a blur. Life out of control and me in the center of it all.

I glance around me, up into Nidia's swirling fog, cloaking our pride. I fantasize about flying into it, escaping with Mom and Tamra.

Only it's just that. A fantasy.

Severin motions and a pair of guards with their loathsome armbands arrive to escort Mom away. 'See that she takes nothing but clothes with her. No gems may leave on her person.'

'Mom!' Tamra screams, then looks desperately to Severin. 'Wait! Please let me talk to her. Just a moment alone—'

'So that she can tell you how to contact her?' Severin shakes his head. 'I'm sorry, but no. As I said, she's a human now, and draki don't consort with humans.' His eyes fall to me as he says this and I don't mistake the accusation there. With a flick of his fingers, Mom is dragged away.

I surge forward but a hard hand on my arm stops me. I try to meet Mom's gaze. Communicate something, glean something from her. Where will she go? What will she do? How will I ever find her again?

Will I ever find her again?

'Bring forth the cutters.'

This command stirs those around me. More blurring movement, more murmuring voices. I crane my neck, but can't see Mom anymore—can't find her in the flurry of activity.

Both my arms are seized and I'm dragged toward a block I notice for the first time, positioned a few feet away on the dais. No one pays attention to my sister when she begs them to stop.

I'm forced to my knees atop the wooden surface.

Apparently they want no one to miss the spectacle. And that's the way of the pride, I realize. At least as long as Severin is alpha. Rule through fear, through intimidation, through threats, both spoken and indirect. This is Severin's way and will continue as long as he's in charge.

I'm commanded to manifest.

I lift my chin, glare straight ahead. They can't make me.

The command comes louder. Still, I don't oblige them. Why make it easy?

Grim satisfaction swells inside me as Severin's face grows splotchy red with anger. He drops heavily beside me, reminding me of his strength and power.

He speaks hard words into my ear, his large hand coming down on the back of my head. 'I'm certain I can get your sister to manifest. She's so untried. It would be an easy thing to inspire fear in her. So what's it going to be? You? Or Tamra? Either way someone's getting her wings clipped today.' I turn and stare into his face, hatred for him emanating from me in waves of heat.

I whisper hoarsely, 'You wouldn't—'

His fingers press deep against my skull. 'She can still serve her purpose *flightless.*'

Staring into his black eyes, I don't know whether he's bluffing or not. But I'm not going to take the chance. I shake off his touch.

I say nothing. I won't give him the gratification of hearing my agreement. I draw a deep breath and manifest.

My human flesh fades out so quickly I don't have time to shed my shirt before my wings are pushing free, tearing the fabric with a terrible sound that mimics the rapid stretching and crackling of my bones.

My injured wing quakes, drooping low. It looks broken. Already clipped. A mirthless smile twists my lips. No one cares. It's about to be crushed anyway.

Even so, it's probably my fastest manifest. Rage and fear speed it along. I tremble from both. Rage at Severin's power. Fear for what I'm about to endure. The acrid taste of it laces every sip of breath.

If I wasn't grasped by both arms, I probably would have lost my balance and fallen off the block.

Terror arcs through me in waves of flashing heat. I can only feel this. Live this now. Endure . . .

Someone arrives bearing the cutters, and then this is all I can see. The glint of the blades inching toward me. They look like large hedge clippers. They look painful.

The crowd is a deafening roar now, a mix of cheering encouragement and sharp protest. At least I think I hear a few shouts of protest. I want to think not everyone agrees I deserve such a punishment. Not everyone hungers for my blood.

My sister's screams and curses burn my ears, and I know she's there, tormented at what's happening.

What's about to happen.

I can't help it. I call for her even though I know she can't help me.

No one can.

She screams my name again and again. Tears stream down my cheeks, hissing on my overheated flesh.

Then, in the mad frenzy, I see Cassian's face, his deep eyes, stark and alive on me. He's on the dais now, where he shouldn't be, shoving his way through the elders to reach me.

I remember then. Hear his deep voice from weeks ago promising to protect me. Or at least try. Does he think he can now? It's too late.

Only he doesn't dive for me. He presses close to his father, seizing his arm through his voluminous robe and speaking furiously, his lips moving fast, the color high in his olive-hued cheeks as he motions wildly to me.

I can't hear his words over the din, but I see that Severin is listening . . . and then he looks at me again, his gaze thoughtful, considering.

I cry out as I'm forced to turn around and present my back to the pride. My gaze darts wildly, seeing nothing but the front double doors of the meeting hall before me.

This is it.

Hands grasp my wings, stretch the wiry-thin membrane uncomfortably taut. I gasp at how much this hurts my injured wing.

I compress my lips and steam escapes my nostrils. Fingers poke and prod, searching for the best place to cut. Bile surges in my throat. I feel violated, ravaged, from the rough groping.

Instinctively, fire surges to the back of my throat, ready to defend, to protect myself. I bite my lip until the taste of blood flows over my teeth. Coppery sweet, it mingles with the flavor of char and ash.

A hard hand shoves my head down until my chin touches my chest. The pose forces my back into a high curve. My wings stretch tall above me, on display, the fiery gossamer sheets poised for the perfect cut.

I hiss, tremble violently as the first cold tip of steel touches one of the wiry tendons latticing my right wing.

The hands on my arms grip harder, squeeze until I can't feel the blood in my biceps . . .

'Don't move,' a voice warns. 'I'd hate to take off your entire wing.'

I choke on a sob and hold still. Then I'm free.

No one touches me anymore. No cold steel kisses my wing, ready to break and sever . . .

I stumble off the block. Fall to the concrete. Tears sting my eyes, clouding the vision of Cassian standing above me, looking down at me with unnaturally bright eyes, his chest lifting on heated breaths.

Severin's voice booms across the air, silencing the rumblings of the pride. 'An alternative to the wing clipping has been proposed and deemed acceptable.'

My head whips in the direction of Severin. Hope springs in my heart and I can only think that I'll do it. Whatever it is. Any alternative would be better.

What could be worse than being hobbled, potentially crippled for life?

'Should Jacinda agree to enter into bonding on this day with Cassian she shall be spared . . .'

All heat drains from my body. I'm cold inside.

I rise shakily, stand distant and still as any statue overlooking the sea of stunned faces. However, none more stunned than mine.

My gaze finds Cassian. His eyes are as cold as I feel inside, black with no hint of light. No wind. No sky. Nothing.

His lips press into a flat line as if to stop himself from explaining why he has done this.

I search his face, looking, seeking something, trying to understand, trying to find the answer there.

This? This is what he offered to his father as a solution? Why has he done this? Does he truly want to bond with me? Or is he just making the grand sacrifice? He doesn't look happy about it . . . about forfeiting himself to save me.

'She agrees,' Cassian announces, staring into my eyes, daring me to disagree. Because he knows I can't. Not with the alternative before me.

No one waits for me to confirm Cassian's claim. I'm whisked away. The elders thrust me into the arms of their mates, females ever happy to serve only them and the pride. The very thing they expect me to become. Complacent. Dutiful. I almost laugh at this image. That could never be me.

I crane my head, look to my right as I descend the steps, trying to catch a glimpse of Tamra's face, *needing* to see her.

Ice shoots to my heart when I finally do. Everything about her is a wash of paleness. Her hair. Her face. Even her eyes are colorless, clear frost. Her lips part, sag slightly open with words that don't emerge.

And Mom. In the nightmare of the last moments, I forgot about her. I look for her, but of course she is gone. Her banishment hasn't been revoked just because I've been spared. *Spared*. Have I really?

I lock eyes with Tamra as I'm swept past, trying to convey to her that I'm sorry, that I don't want this to happen, that it won't happen. It *won't*.

But as I'm borne away I realize that's a lie. I can't stop any of this.

Maybe I've been kidding myself to think that I can control anything—that I could ever avoid the fate the pride chose for me long ago.

23

The night is quiet, even with so many surrounding me on every side. This mist seems darker, more gray than its usual chalky white, and I wonder if this has to do with Tamra's mood.

I'm led to the flight field. Tall grasses ripple against my legs as we move to the center. The mountains sit in silent witness, great jagged shapes splashed against the skyline.

Garbed in a lush amber cloak, I feel like the proverbial lamb being led to the slaughter. When we arrive at the site where generations of draki have been bonded, I locate the titanium-edged circle on the ground. Not difficult to do. The sapphires outlining it glow in the night, a beautiful blue, mesmerizing. Only sapphires, one of the strongest stones on earth, edge the circle of titanium. The ring symbolizes the unbreakable union between two draki.

I look away from the circle even as I'm guided toward it. They position me just outside it. Cassian already waits on the other side of the ring, wearing a cloak of shimmering black. I stare for a moment at his face, fully manifested as I am.

The pride is silent, watching raptly.

I don't look around me. I don't look for Tamra, but I know she is here. Watching alongside everyone else as I prepare to bond with Cassian. I feel her eyes on me.

Hands remove our cloaks, and we're directed to drink from the ceremonial chalice.

My lips hug the edge of the goblet that generations of draki sipped from to seal their bonds. My own parents. I blink burning eyes. This is harder than I imagined. Doing this and then telling myself it doesn't mean anything is harder to believe than I thought.

It isn't a true bonding. I don't enter the bond freely, so it doesn't count.

Except I remember my mother's words, *Something happens, something changes, when you're bonded in that circle, Jacinda.*

Was she right? Would this change things? Will's face rises in my mind. I can't let this ceremony take any piece of him from me and replace it with Cassian. I can't. I *won't.*

I lick the last drop of wine from my lips and watch as Cassian drinks from the jeweled chalice, his lips touching the same edge from which I sipped.

Severin speaks, but I deliberately block out his words, his voice. I've attended bonding ceremonies before. I know what he's saying. I don't want to hear him speak the words.

Then it appears. My family's cache of jewels.

I fight down the sudden lump in my throat and stare hard at the lockbox, thinking of the amber stone already lost from it—sold away when we were in Chaparral. I feel a surge of possession as an elder's hand delves inside, riffling among the contents. It's not his right. Usually a parent of the bonded couple does this, but in this case I'm without a parent.

Cassian's gems are next. His father digs inside their family's box.

The gems are pulled free at the same time. I blink at the beautiful black pearl removed from Cassian's box. Perfectly round, it fills his father's palm. An amber piece is selected from my family's cache. I distinctly remember every gem in that box and know it to be the last amber left. I know why they chose this one. It's the stone that most represents me.

The amber and pearl are held high in the air, displayed before the pride. A gem from each of our family's caches. Two gems to begin our legacy together. Our own family.

The lump in my throat grows and no matter how hard I try, I can't swallow it.

Together, united, the two stones project a different glow, a different energy altogether. I hear their whispering song and watch as they are placed in a new box. Black lacquer with fiery red coiled carvings etched on top of the lid. This one is ours. Mine and Cassian's. And I wonder how long ago it was made in preparation for this moment.

Then it's time. We must begin our ascent. Our last flight as independent individuals.

Eyes locked, we lift off the ground and soar. I ignore the twinge in my injured wing and lift, lift, lift.

Face angled into the cool, wet wind, I luxuriate in the taste of sky again—despite myself. Despite wanting to like nothing about this moment. Flying has always been my balm. I can't resist the sweetness of it . . . not after knowing I almost lost this when I came so close to a wing clipping.

My wings work, slap the air, take me higher and higher. It's as though I'm racing away from it all, straining to get as far from the pride as possible. I close my eyes, savor the speeding wind rushing against my face.

For a moment, the thought flashes through my mind to just keep going, melt away, vanish into the sky. Never come down. At least not on pride grounds.

Then I see Cassian, winding through the mist and clouds with me. His great wings gleam darker than the night, powerful sails of onyx with winking undertones of purple.

His gaze holds mine as we twist and twirl upward. And I know. He knows my thoughts. He knows but his face reveals nothing.

And then I understand. Feel it deep in my chest where fire and char dwells.

He would let me go. Escape into the night, disappear into the sifting mist and clouds.

The choice is in my hands.

I imagine this. Imagine him drifting back down to the pride without me. Facing everyone, shamed and abandoned. Of course, they would come after me. I probably wouldn't get very far. Not much of a chance, really.

Suddenly, he stops. Floats adrift.

I stop, too, buoyed on the air.

I face him. Several inches separate us. Night clouds drift below us, above us. Cold vaporous wisps float around us like chilled smoke.

I catch glimpses of his face through breaks of cloudy air. A flash of shimmering charcoal, eyes like obsidian.

'It won't be real,' I call to him. My voice is swept up in the wind, and I'm not sure he heard me until he calls back:

'It'll be real enough.'

Real enough? For him? Is that what he's saying? Does he think a bond where only one of us is fully committed will be fulfilling? To either one of us? Or is he holding out for that connection to form and tie us together?

I've already lost so much this day. Will. Mom. I glance down. Tamra waits there, far below, as betrayed as I am by the pride.

I raise my gaze back to Cassian. *It won't be real. This won't be real.*

I swim through air toward him. It's the only answer he needs.

For now, this is what I must do. What the moment demands.

His eyes soften as we embrace, do what draki have done down through the millennia. His hands rest gently where they touch me. One at my back between my wings, the other on my hip. For all that, his stare is no less intense, drilling into me as if he were memorizing everything about my face, everything about this moment.

I close my eyes and try to forget. Think only of Will. That I'll see him again.

Cassian's body is rock solid against mine, and I remember that he's bred to be a warrior. Tough and unyielding, but I feel safe in his arms, not the least threatened by his power, his strength.

Plastered against each other, we begin our descent. My stomach falls, pitches to my feet. It's like the dream, the nightmare. I'm falling, unable to lift up. To catch myself.

I'm falling and there is no help for it.

Where we ascended as two, we descend as one. That's the bonding act. That is what we must do. What this is all about.

I'd always thought the bonding rite romantic, something special I would share with someone one day. Even so, it loomed far away. A distant prospect. But now it's real. It's happening to me right now.

Cassian's arms hold me as we plummet. Air roars past as we twist in a speeding circle, dropping, hurtling to earth. My hair flies up from my scalp. Even Cassian's hair tears from his face and flutters like dark ribbons from his head.

We stare at each other, nose to nose, the howl of the wind loud as a freight train in our ears as we twist and spiral toward the pride waiting below.

It's not just *him* holding *me*. I clutch him closely. Our legs tangle and slip between each other's.

It's as if we are actually cleaving to each other in this moment . . . as if we're diving toward our deaths. And I guess that's the point. The act is meant to symbolize the death of our independent selves and the start of our union as one.

I don't breathe. Can't even if I wished to. We move at an incomprehensible speed, the air too fast to draw into my constricting lungs.

Suddenly, the clouds ease and clear. The mist and fog loosens. Inches before crashing into the earth's hard skin, we spread our wings, pull up and set down gently within the ring of stones.

Together. In each other's arms. Draki bonded.

* * *

I don't spot my sister anywhere during the festivities that follow. I'm constantly surrounded, toasted, plied with food and well wishes.

As if I did not stand at the block a short time ago with cutters at my back. Now I've proven myself. Bonding with Cassian convinces my pride, at last, that I'm one of them. Even if they don't fully trust me yet, they trust the bonding process . . . and they trust Cassian.

Through the festivities, I search for Tamra, but find no sight of her.

I *need* to see her. Need to make sure she's all right. That *we* are. My face feels tight, eyes achy.

'Come,' Cassian murmurs, rising from the long table where we sit. His large hand encloses mine, the palm work-roughened against my skin. 'It's late.'

Over merry protests we leave the celebration together. But not before I spot Severin, drinking and smiling. Apparently his thoughts for his daughter are forgotten. His gaze meets mine and he lifts his glass in silent toast, happy to have me in his family, in his grasp at last.

He thinks he's won. That I'm beaten.

'Leaving already?' Corbin steps in our path.

'Jacinda's tired. She's had a long day,' Cassian replies in a voice that reveals nothing.

Corbin glares at his cousin, his pupils vibrating slits. 'And I'm sure you're eager to tuck her in.'

My breath escapes in a hiss. Alarm fills me as the implication sinks in. Cassian and I are bonded now.

'Watch your mouth,' Cassian warns, his voice thick, his hand around mine tightening faintly. His anger comes to me full force, heavy as a great gust of fog. And it's more than anger. It's possession, *need*.

I flinch at the bombarding sensations and tug my hand from his, desperate to sever the contact, anything to lessen the link between us. Is this it then? What Mom spoke of? The connection? Are we forever each other's emotional barometer? *Great*.

Corbin smiles widely and steps aside. 'Of course.'

Reclaiming my hand, Cassian walks a hard line past his cousin, leading us away.

I follow him, sealing myself in a cocoon of numbness, hoping to keep him out—and me in. My legs move automatically. Only when we step on my porch, do I realize where we are.

'This is my house,' I say.

'My father said we're to live here.'

I blink and glance around. I'll live with Cassian here? At the home I grew up in?

And then I get it. No one else lives here anymore. No more Dad. Tamra's with Nidia. Severin saw to it that Mom is out of the picture. It's just me here. And now my bonded mate.

I stare at the front door like I don't know it. And I guess I don't. The house is no longer mine. It's Cassian's now. And by extension Severin's, too.

A strange new world waits on the other side. A future with Cassian.

My stomach rebels, roils with acid. No. My future isn't this. It's not something foisted upon me. My future is mine. Something of my choosing. Something, I realize, that includes Will. I know that now more than ever.

I shake my head. How could I have told him that we didn't belong together? He's *it*—the one. The only one. No matter what he is, what I am . . .

I'll find a way to be with him again.

Cassian opens the door and together we enter the house.

24

Despite the late hour, I take a bath, letting the warm water ease and soothe my tired and abused muscles. I linger, soaking in the water long after my skin shrivels to a prune, and I admit to myself that it's more than relaxation holding me hostage in the bathroom.

I hear nothing outside the door. Rising from the water, I dry off and dress, leaving the sanctuary of the bathroom, ready to face Cassian. A hundred different words burn on my tongue, ready to spill free.

I peer inside my bedroom, glad to find him not there. With a shuddery breath, I move down the hall into the living room. He unfolds himself from the couch when I enter the room.

His gaze glides over me, lingering on the wet fall of my hair. Before I can say anything, he asks, 'Which room do you want me to have?'

I blink even though that's so very Cassian. Straight to the point.

He continues, 'I imagine you'll still want to sleep in your room. I can take Tamra's or your mom's room.'

Relief floods through me. I can't deny that I worried about this moment, wondering at his expectations. Wondering at my reaction to him with this new . . . *thing* between us.

'T-Tamra's room,' I supply. Having him spend his nights in my sister's room strikes me as somehow fitting.

We remain standing where we are, staring at each other, neither moving. And yet words fly, unspoken between us. I fumble with my hands, ending up twisting my fingers until they're numb, bloodless.

There's so much I don't understand—why he's doing this, why he's not pushing the matter of intimacy now that we're bonded. I'm no idiot. Even though I didn't agree to anything, I know that certain expectations come with the act of bonding. We're taught the importance of procreation from day one in primary school. The pride must live on.

In the kitchen the ice maker rumbles and I nearly jump at the sudden sound. His eyes dart around like an uneasy bird, looking for a place to land. He's nervous, too, I realize—or maybe I *sense* it. A definite first. I've never seen Cassian nervous before.

I guess I should thank him, express my gratitude to him for saving me from the wing clipping. The words stick in my throat.

He finally clears his throat. The sound is loud and startling. 'I know it will take time for this to seem real to you.'

I can only stare. *Time?* He thinks time will help me accept? Does a prisoner, an inmate, ever grow accustomed to his cell? Or maybe he thinks in time I'll start to confuse our *connection* for something else? Something more?

'I know you're worried about tonight.'

Of course. We're connected. He knows the fears stumbling through me, making me jump out of my skin.

'I'll give you time, Jacinda. I can be patient. We have plenty of time for . . . whatever feels right.'

So I'll have a reprieve then. But for how long? How long can I keep him at arm's length? Oh, Cassian would never force the issue, but how long can I fake that we're a truly bonded couple before the watchful eyes of the pride? Before Severin.

How long before I cave and do what's easy, forgetting what I truly want . . . who I truly am? Forgetting Will.

Will's face materializes in my mind, and the answer comes to me clearly. *Never.*

I don't have to pretend we're *truly* bonded for very long at all. I inhale a fortifying breath. One week. Just one week and I'll be free.

Slipping into bed, I sigh, appreciating the comforting familiarity of my plump pillow. The down-stuffed comforter that smells faintly of lavender surrounds me and reminds me of Mom. The stars on my ceiling glow, even all these years later. They're still here. Even when Dad is not. How did this happen? How have I lost so much? Dad. Mom.

I turn my face into the pillow and release a ragged cry into its depths. Not Will, though. I won't lose him, too. And I won't lose my sister.

Tomorrow. I'll find Tamra and tell her everything. *Everything.* No more secrets.

I'll tell her about Will's plan to wait outside the pride for me a week from now. I'll ask her to join me when I meet him. I'll ask her to run away with us. Come with us wherever we go. We can find Mom.

I tremble a little at the prospect, a little frightened at confessing so many secrets to her . . . frightened that I might lose her, too. I couldn't stand that.

I clutch the pillow tighter, trying to convince myself that it won't happen. Tamra has to be disillusioned enough with the pride to agree to leave. They banished Mom. Almost clipped my wings. And now the only draki she's wanted for her own is bonded to me. How could she want to stay?

I rub my cheek against the pillow, my hand slipping beneath it—fingers brushing the crisp edge of paper.

Heart thundering in my chest, I close my hand around the slip of paper. Sitting up, I flip on the lamp, anxiously brushing the wet tangle of hair from my eyes so I can see.

It's just a small scrap really. Something ripped off from an old envelope. Four words stare up at me, written hurriedly in Mom's scrawling hand.

Remember the Palm Tree

It's a clue. A hint. I hug the paper to my chest, my eyes straining in the gloom of my room. Mom left this for me. She's trying to tell me where she's going. *Where I can find her!*

And it makes absolutely no sense to me.

Still, it gives me hope. A corner of my mouth starts to curl. Mom's out there, waiting for me. She wouldn't have written this down unless she thought I could figure it out.

I tighten my fingers around the slip of paper. I'll remember. Or Tamra will. And together we'll find our mother. I'm not beaten. Severin hasn't won.

I don't see Tamra the next day. Or the one after that. The week creeps along, and with it my anxiety grows, something dark and shadowy filling my heart.

I forgot it was custom for newly bonded couples to sequester themselves in their house, seeing no one, doing nothing but better *acquainting* themselves with their new lives together. A honeymoon, of sorts. It's expected among the pride. Severin expected it, and since I had vowed to act the dutiful submissive, I have no choice but to play my part.

Members of the pride come and go, never announcing themselves. I hear their footsteps, their whispers in front of the house as they leave food and gifts on the porch. Anything and everything to make our time together special.

On our last day of forced solitude I step out on the porch to collect a basket of fresh-baked breads and muffins that I spotted Nidia leaving earlier, and also a pitcher of lemonade someone else had dropped off.

With the basket looped around my arm and the pitcher hugged against me, I catch movement across the street. I hold still and spot the source.

Corbin leans against a post on his porch, his arms folded across his chest. He stares at me as he always has. Smug and determined.

I shake my head and start to turn. It doesn't make sense why he would still look at me that way. Not after I've bonded to Cassian. We're nothing to each other. Now he has to know that. Now he has to give up his stupid obsession.

Then Jabel steps onto their porch and calls for him. When she sees Corbin staring, she follows his gaze and frowns.

Her voice floats from across the street, ringing with censure. Bonded couples are supposed to be left alone during this time, and I guess Corbin's intense staring doesn't exactly constitute that.

'Corbin,' she calls, her voice heavier. When her gaze meets mine she gives me a half smile.

I've bonded with Cassian. In her eyes I've reaffirmed my commitment to the pride. I'm part of her family now. Maybe that lessens the sting of losing Miram.

She orders Corbin inside. Still, he doesn't move. Just looks at me in that consuming way of his that creeps me out. But now I'm bonded to his cousin, beyond his reach.

So why? He doesn't know it's all a farce. He can't know that. And yet he stares.

I turn and go inside, my flesh prickling, still feeling his watchful gaze.

Cassian and I eat together in silence, our last meal alone. Then I catch myself and realize all the remaining nights this week will be like this. Him. Me. Alone.

We'll go our separate ways during the day, performing our duties, socializing, living. But our nights are reserved for each other. My skin shivers, heat crawling deep beneath the skin.

Until, of course, I make my escape.

'Do you have plans for tomorrow?'

'I'm going to see my sister,' I answer truthfully, before I can think that maybe I shouldn't bring up Tamra.

He nods, scrapes the tines of his fork along his plate. 'Maybe I should come with you—'

'I don't think that's a good idea,' I quickly say.

He nods again, slowly, processing. 'OK.'

I stab a piece of fish on my plate. I don't need him hanging around when I tell my sister that I plan to run away with Will and want her to come with us.

'For now,' he adds.

I look up, frowning. 'What do you mean?'

He continues, 'I can't hide from your sister forever. We have to make things right.'

'You think that can happen?' I ask, staring intently at him. 'That you can make things right with Tamra?'

He grimaces, shifts in his chair across from me. 'I hope so. She's your sister and I'm your . . .'

I stare at him, my gaze sharp, cutting. Don't say it. *We're not that.* You're not my *chosen* mate.

'We're family now. All of us.'

I say nothing. Gripping my plate, I rise and enter the kitchen and start on the dishes with feverish intensity.

Cassian joins me. Side by side, I wash and he dries. We work silently, fall into a rhythm. I wince as I think of my parents doing this same thing for years, standing in this very spot. Bonded. *Connected.*

Only we're not my parents. Not even close. We don't laugh and talk. We don't share stories about our day. I don't allow that. I feel a certain sadness drifting off him and settling deeply into me, mingling with my own heartache for Will and Mom. And this only makes me madder. I shouldn't have to feel his emotions. I have enough of my own to cope with.

As we perform our mundane task, I think about tomorrow. When I'll see Tamra again. When we can talk about how we will leave this world behind forever. A world that steals from you and gives nothing in return.

25

Irise early and don't bother with breakfast. No sound comes from Cassian's room as I slip from the house. I rush through the township, through streets that are mostly bare, the dawn air thick as chalk dust, still and silent except for my thundering tread and gasping breath.

As I hurry down Main, my spirits lift when Nidia's cottage comes into view. Then my elation is crushed.

My heart seizes as Corbin steps into my path, appearing out of nowhere. From behind a hedge, I guess. As though he were lying in wait. He grabs my arm and drags me beneath one of the many evergreens lining the lower half of Main. He presses me against the rough bark, trapping me between the massive tree and his body.

'Take your hands off me,' I hiss. My body reacts instantly, instinct kicking in. Fire erupts at my core, smolder eating up my throat. The taste of ash and char coats my mouth.

'Let's get something straight.'

I don't listen, don't care to hear whatever it is he has to say.

Shaking with fury, I glare down at his hands on my arms. Emotion sweeps over me in a hot burn. 'You dare touch me? Cassian will kill—'

'Oh, very affecting. I'm impressed. I almost believe you and Cassian are a true couple instead of the charade you're playing at.'

Cold sweeps through me, dousing my heat. 'W-what do you mean?'

Corbin leans in, brushes his nose to my cheek, and inhales sharply. I cringe at the contact and blink once, hard. 'I know the truth,' he whispers, his voice a harsh rasp in my ear. 'You're not his. You've never been his. You've always held yourself from him. Bonding with him hasn't changed that.'

I open my mouth to deny this, but can't. I can't say the words, can't insist that Cassian and I are in love. Saying those words, with Will in my heart . . . I just *can't*. Whether it's good for me or not. Instead I growl, 'Get away from me.'

'I'd see it in your eyes. He'd be a part of you. But you're the same. Unchanged.'

It's strange, but I almost hope he's right.

His eyes glint, flash down at me. 'Still untouched.' He smiles then, a cruel twist of his lips. 'Which means there's still a chance for us.'

I snort. 'You're crazy.'

'Keep telling yourself that. Only I know the truth, and soon everyone else will, too. If I have to singlehandedly make them see it. I'll prove it. And then I'll be there to do what my cousin is too much of a coward to do.'

I can't breathe as I stare up into his face. If I didn't know I needed to get away—far away—this would only confirm it. Corbin is crazy enough to do just what he says.

He inches his head closer . . . like he's actually going to kiss me. 'I'll still claim you.'

I don't think. Just react. I part my lips and release the burn that froths at my core, making my skin contract and snap fiercely.

Steam pours from my lips in a thin ribbon. Satisfaction swells inside me as the hot vapor scalds him. He howls, clutching the right side of his face. I seize my opportunity and squeeze out from between him and the tree.

I run the rest of the way to Nidia's, his shouts chasing after me.

'It's you and me, Jacinda. I'm going to own you! You can't run forever!'

I jerk to a hard stop at Nidia's door and resist the urge to pound the wood with my fist. It's still early. No sense beating the door as if wild wolves were chasing me.

I rest one hand against the door, the other to my heart, gathering my breath. When the door pulls opens, I stop just short of falling forward.

Tamra stands there, her red-rimmed eyes inscrutable, but I know she's hurting as much as I am.

'Let's run away,' I blurt. Just like that. No easing in, no working up to it.

Holding my breath, I wait and hope I'm not off base to think she'll even consider the risky venture. That she'll even want to surrender her newfound status with the pride. It feels like forever as I wait for her to answer me, to speak, to say anything.

'How soon can we leave?'

I release a ragged breath, almost weep from the relief— and then I realize the tricky part is still left. I have to explain Will.

I glance over my shoulder, making sure Corbin is gone, and then I turn around and glance pointedly inside the house. Tamra quickly motions me in and leads me to her room—what was once Nidia's spare room. The bedroom doesn't bear her mark yet. She's transferred very little from her old room at our house into it. Even Nidia's sewing table still occupies one side.

I sit on the unmade bed, the covers a wild tangle beneath me.

She closes the door softly. 'So how are we going to do this?'

I brace myself and meet her gaze and say the one word that should explain it all. 'Will.'

She stares at me for several moments and then asks in a surprisingly even voice. 'Have you been seeing him?'

I nod.

'The day Miram and you . . .' Her voice fades. Sucking in a breath, she asks what I've been dreading, 'Were you meeting Will then?'

Again, I nod. She sighs, and the sound is tired.

'I left you and Mom notes, but Miram took them, and she followed me. Then the hunters came . . .'

She shakes her head.

'Are you very angry?' I ask quietly.

'I don't know. Maybe. I'm so tired. Tired of being mad. I just want to leave here. Find Mom and never come back.' The pain in her voice makes me feel even worse. Because I put it there. At least partly. And because I can't promise her peace. At least not yet.

'There's something I have to do before we can find Mom. I was hoping you would help me.' With her particular talent, Tamra's assistance could be the difference between life and death.

Wariness fills her smoky gaze. 'What?'

'I'm going to rescue Miram.' And then I'd be square with the pride. With Cassian. With *myself.*

Her eyes widen. 'Miram? But isn't she with the enkros?'

I nod. 'But they won't have killed her yet. I don't think. Not for a while. They'll want to do some'—I shy from the foulness of the word *experimenting* and substitute— 'observing.'

'So you think you can just march into wherever they have her and ask nicely for them to hand her over?'

I angle my head and say slowly, 'No, but I think I can bust her out. With Will's help. And yours. I owe her that.' And Cassian, I can't help thinking.

'You *owe* her? Miram? She's never been anything but a jerk.'

'She never would have been taken if I hadn't been out there waiting for Will.'

Tamra digests this, looking me over appraisingly.

'Look,' I say, 'let's just make it to their stronghold, check it out . . . and then we'll see.' I bite my lip, hoping she can't read my thoughts. That once I have the enkros stronghold in sight, I'm going in. No way I'm backing out. I'm getting Miram free . . . and I just might do a little damage in the process. My blood warms at this, and I feel stronger, fortified. The idea of taking the entire operation down gives me a decided rush.

'All right,' she agrees, but the hesitation is there, clear in her voice, reminding me of every time I dragged her into a scheme that she didn't really want to do.

'Mom left a note,' I say, happy to give her some bit of good news.

221

Her eyes brighten. 'Where? What did it say?'

'I destroyed it. Didn't want anyone to find it, but it said "Remember the palm tree."'

'"Remember the palm tree"? What's that mean?'

Disappointment stabs me. Tamra doesn't remember either. 'I don't know, but she obviously thought it would mean something to us. I'm sure we can figure it out.'

'Yeah.' She nods, and her voice sounds stronger, less miserable, and I'm so vastly relieved Mom left a clue, a life raft in a turbulent sea. Something, anything, to hang on to. Tamra's steady gaze rests on me. 'When do we go?'

'Will is supposed to meet me in three days.'

'Three days,' she murmurs, looking disappointed. 'And then we have to find Miram and bring her back here before searching for Mom? We're really going to keep Mom hanging like that? For a girl we don't even like?'

'Well, we don't know what Mom's note means yet. We don't know where to go. And Mom would know we might not get to slip away soon. She won't give up on us.'

Tamra's gaze narrows on me. 'So you're supposed to live with Cassian for three more days?' Her accusing voice claws through me. Like this is something I've done deliberately. Something I want. It's the first time she's mentioned Cassian. It's more than awkward talking about the boy she's obsessed over for her whole life—who happens to be bonded to me now.

My mind flashes to the cold press of those cutters on my wings. The memory echoes through me and I can taste the fear like I'm there again. Up on that block. Has she forgotten that?

One side of her mouth curls as she adds, 'That should be cozy.'

'It's not . . .' I wet my lips. 'It's not like that.'

Her stare penetrates and I pluck at the edge of a twist-ed sheet, thinking I need to choose my words carefully. I can read the question in her eyes. *What is it like then?*

'He hasn't . . . *we* haven't done anything . . . irrevers-ible.'

Her lips twist. 'No? I thought he would be most eager to—'

'Yeah, well, I'm not.' I'm not eager for anyone but Will.

'Right.' And I know what she's thinking. Why her voice carries that mocking edge. She's remembering that moment she interrupted us. How close we stood. Cas-sian's hand on my face. And she doesn't even know we've actually *kissed*. Guilty heat swamps over me.

I cross my arms over my chest. 'He sleeps in one room and I'm in the other, and that's the way it's going to stay until you and I get out of here.'

She looks away, stares through her bedroom window at the ivy-covered wall. Not much of a view. 'How are we going to get past the guard on duty?'

I hadn't thought that far ahead yet. I'd been too busy worrying about whether Tamra would agree to escape with me or not.

And then I know what to do. 'A distraction,' I murmur.

'Yeah? What?'

'Not what. *Who*.'

26

Az's laughter floats on the air like softly ringing bells. Tamra and I wait anxiously, tucked away, out of sight, squatting low behind Nidia's house.

The sudden loss of the sound prompts us to move. As one we peer around the edge of the house. Sure enough, she's locking lips with fifteen-year-old Remy. The boy is stuck like glue to Az. His hands grip her back like he fears the older girl might vanish from his arms.

Backpacks slung over our shoulders, we sneak past them and out the entrance. I glance over my shoulder. Az watches us, her bright eyes wide-open, urging us on even as I know she's sad for us to go.

With a farewell wave, I charge ahead. My breath escapes my lips in hot puffs. Any moment I expect to hear the alarm. I wait for draki to spill out from the township and catch us.

In such an event, I could expect the worst punishment. I doubt it would stop at a wing clipping. Severin's wrath will be all the mightier for me taking Tamra away, too . . . for leaving them without their next shader.

The pride—Severin—would know I didn't honor my bond to Cassian. Corbin would be quick to point that out. I shiver and dart a glance at my sister.

She catches my gaze and gives me a small smile as we leap over a fallen log, in perfect accord as we flee. That feels good. To be together in this. It's too bad that it's such a mess bringing us together.

Our feet thud softly over damp earth. We cut through nourishing mists, weaving through trees we know well.

I pull ahead of Tamra, eager to leave the pride behind, hungry for the sight of Will.

I feel him first.

Before I even break through the trees, I know he's there from the snap of my skin, the sudden quivering heat in my throat.

And then I see him.

I stop, panting hard, my gaze devouring him. He looks back at me, and there's the barest surprise there—in his face.

He didn't think I would come, and now here I stand with a bulging backpack, all humming eagerness, my face and eyes telling him all he needs to know.

It's unclear who moves first. We're in each other's arms, lips locked, melded, hotly fused. Our hands drag over each other, reacquainting, remembering, almost as if we're both verifying the other one is real flesh and blood. His fingers catch in the snarls of my hair and I kiss him harder, catch my teeth on his lip.

He makes a small sound into my mouth and it ripples through me, undoing me. Making me forget everything but *this*. His lips on mine.

Tamra clears her throat. Will jumps from me and yanks me behind him. I smile, my heart lightening at the protective gesture, even if it's unnecessary.

I wrap my fingers around his arm. 'It's all right. Tamra's coming with us.'

'Tamra?'

I nod. 'Yeah. I'll explain it all later. We better go. Before they notice we've left.'

Nodding, Will slips his hand around mine and starts toward the Land Rover.

'Don't tell me this is your human. The same one Nidia shaded?'

I stop cold at the voice.

Turning slowly, I drop Will's hand and brace myself.

Fire erupts inside me as Corbin steps from the trees. There's no smile on his face, but satisfaction gleams in his eyes.

'I knew you'd slip up. And I'd be there when it happened.' His gaze flicks to Will. 'So this is why you won't give any of us poor draki guys the time of day.'

Tamra says my name hesitantly, her eyes confused. 'Jacinda?'

I wave her to silence, my gaze fixed on Corbin, swallowing in a bitter wash what his being here means. What I'll have to do to ensure our escape. My hands flex at my sides. 'You shouldn't have followed us.'

'Oh, clearly I should have. My uncle will reward me well for stopping the pride's fire-breather and shader from escaping.' His nostrils flare deeply and his purply black gaze scours me. 'Even Cassian can't save you now. You're not his anymore. You're mine—just like I said you would be.'

226

Will's voice cracks over the air then, and there is nothing hesitant about it. 'Touch her and I'll kill you.' The words thrum on the air, menacing and dark as the predator I first met months ago, in these very woods.

It seems ridiculous, on principle, that one human could defeat a strong onyx like Corbin. But then I remember. Will's not an average human. He's something more . . . something not to be underestimated.

Corbin's eyes snap to Will, his face vicious and hateful as he gazes at his centuries-old enemy. His human flesh blurs, fades out in a flash. His hands grasp his shirt and he tears it from his body in a violent rip, revealing his charcoal-dark flesh. Sinew ripples as he springs into the air.

Will squares off, ready for the hit, but I dive before him and unleash the heat simmering inside me. Not yet manifested, only a blast of steam escapes me, not actual fire. And even that's wasted. Corbin dodges the steam. He flies behind me before I can turn on him. I cry out as he kicks me hard in the back.

I hit the ground. The impact is brutal, jarring me to the teeth. My chin scrapes earth. Coughing, I spit up dirt and blood. Tamra drops, crouches near me to help me back up.

A roar fills the air, wrenches at something deep inside me.

I watch as Will launches himself high enough in the air to grab on to Corbin's legs and drag him down to the ground.

Corbin curses, smacking his wings as he tries to lift back up, but Will is tenacious, pulling him to earth with all his strength. They crash down in a tangle of limbs and slapping wings.

227

Once on the ground, Will straddles Corbin and starts pummeling him, swinging punch after punch. The crunch of bone on bone fills the air, a sickening sound. I watch, forgetting the pain in my chin, feeling only the cruel twist of my heart. Heat builds inside my chest and rises up into my mouth.

Corbin writhes, and soon they're rolling, a speeding blur, until they look like one wild shape.

Corbin finally breaks free, sweeping up into the air. Blood runs from his ridged nose, and his eyes glitter with furious malice. He circles above Will like a hawk, ready to pick apart his prey.

Will crouches, braces himself. Even now his expression is beautiful in its intensity and my heart aches.

Corbin holds up his taloned fingers like claws ready to strike. The nails glint like razors. It's a kill pose.

'Will!' I call out in warning.

Corbin swoops, a streak of black. He jabs and makes contact.

Will cries outs, clutches a hand to his arm. From where Tamra and I huddle, I see several deep gashes, his telltale blood . . . the glisten of purple welling between his fingers.

Corbin sees it, too, snarls in our tongue, 'How many draki have you killed, hunter, so that our blood can flow in your veins?'

'Corbin, no!' I shout.

'Shut up, Jacinda. Watch while I drain every drop of draki blood from him!'

My throat tightens, thickens with fire. My skin snaps and I let go. Feel myself give over to my draki.

I surge from Tamra's side, burst from the confines of my blouse. My wings unfurl as I dive for Corbin, stretch myself to reach him as he lunges for Will, his clawed hands angled for his throat. And I know with a sick twist of my heart—I'm not going to make it.

A scream swells up in my throat, mingling with the fire and smoke. My talonlike fingers extend, reach, grasp only air.

Just as Corbin is about to make contact, Will's hand goes up and a howling wall of dirt surges up between them.

The great wave of dark earth, twigs and shredded grass—nearly as tall as the trees surrounding us—propels Corbin back, flings him several yards through the air and slams him to the ground with crushing force.

I gasp, dropping to the ground and covering my head with my hands to ward off the raining earth. Tamra does the same not far from me. We're not in its direct path, but we still get hit with some of the debris.

Squinting against the clearing cloud of dirt, I find Will, meet his gaze, see the astonishment there that mirrors my own thoughts.

'Look out!' Tamra screams.

Corbin is back up. Blood dribbles from a gash in his head. He touches it lightly and examines his fingers. His expression turns brutal at the evidence of his injury. With a shout, he surges back into the air.

Before Will has a chance to do . . . *whatever it is he did again*, a second streak of black crosses my vision. It's so fast that at first I think it's more debris that Will sent soaring on the wind.

I follow the object, look around wildly, locate it. *Him*. Cassian.

He crashes into Corbin and pins him to the ground.

They strain against each other, ancient creatures, beautiful and wild in their draki forms, all black with quivering leathery wings.

Corbin claws with his hands, grunting. Spittle flies from his lips as he tries to bring his talons across his cousin's throat. I cease to breathe, can only watch.

It all happens so quickly. A mere second . . . but I can't move.

Cassian fumbles one hand on the ground and grabs a large rock. I gasp as he brings it down—clubbing Corbin in the head with a savage blow.

Corbin stills, his head lolling to the side.

I take a hesitant step forward. 'Is he . . . did you . . .'

Panting, the ridges of his nose vibrating, Cassian casts his eyes over his shoulder at me. 'No. He'll come to soon.'

With a heavy breath, he rises in a single fluid motion, his wings great sails behind him, and I realize he's more natural this way, more comfortable as a draki than human. For a time, I felt the same way. Now I don't know what I prefer. What I am more—draki or human.

'Jacinda,' Will says my name, coming up beside me. I reach out and slip my arm around him. Lifting my gaze to Cassian, I let that say everything. Let the gesture speak for itself.

Cassian stares at us both, and I hold his stare, trying not to let anything he may be feeling penetrate and influence me. Still, I pick up a trickle of sentiment from him. Anger. Regret. Sorrow.

The words *I'm sorry* rise to my lips, but I can't let them fall. Can't apologize for the way I feel for Will.

'You're leaving,' he announces in his rough, guttural tongue.

230

In a blink, I demanifest, fold back into my human shape. 'Yes.' Tamra is there, helping me slip my tattered shirt back on.

Still watching me, Cassian follows suit, demanifests and stands before me wearing only a pair of torn jeans. He glances at Tamra. 'She's going, too?'

'I'm right here,' she snaps. 'You don't have to talk about me like I'm not.'

I follow his gaze to my sister. Her eyes spark like shards of ice as she glares at Cassian . . . and I think her infatuation with him might truly be at an end.

'You'll leave the pride?' I'm not sure who he's asking.

'After everything that's happened?' I wave a hand. 'Why would I stay?'

'Because there are things bigger and more important than what you want,' he returns, his gaze flicking meaningfully to Will.

'You're not one to talk about putting aside *wants*.' Tamra's voice is venom. 'You wanted Jacinda and made certain that you got her. That wasn't for the pride. That was for you and no one else.'

'What's she talking about?' Will growls beside me, his hand tightening on mine.

'Do we really want to do this now?' I glare at each of them and motion to Corbin. 'He's liable to wake up any moment and we're too close to pride grounds.'

A muscle feathers across Will's jaw. Still glaring at Cassian, he tugs me toward the truck. 'You're right. Let's get out of here.'

Cassian's voice follows me. 'Run away, Jacinda. You're good at that.'

Will stiffens at my side, but it's Tamra who comes unglued. She spins around, all spitting fury. 'Don't be so self-righteous! You want to know where we're going? And none of us *want* to go there, let me assure you of that. We're going to rescue your brat of a sister who got only what she deserved because she was spying on Jacinda.'

'Miram?' His gaze shoots to me. 'Is that true? You're going to rescue Miram?' His gaze swings to Will. 'She's not dead?'

Will holds silent for a long moment, and I hold my breath. Finally, he answers. 'She lives.'

Something passes over Cassian's eyes. A lightness that had not been there seconds ago. I sense his relief. 'Then I'm going with you.'

'What?' Tamra demands, chasing after him as he stalks toward the vehicle. 'I don't think so!'

'She's my sister,' he returns, his voice tight, his lips barely moving.

Tamra looks helplessly at me and Will, her eyes perfectly communicating her plea: *Don't let him come.*

'It's going to be dangerous,' I warn.

'Jacinda,' Tamra hisses.

Cassian just looks at me, and I realize the threat of danger would hardly discourage him.

I turn to study Will, wait for him to decide. He's leading this mission. I move my thumb against the inside of his wrist in a small circle. He gives my hand a single squeeze and then walks ahead, guiding me to the passenger side. 'We better get out of here.'

With a grim nod, Cassian gets in the back of the Land Rover.

Tamra mutters, but climbs in, too, making certain to stay as far from him as possible.

Will starts the car, slipping one hand over mine as he steers us from the clearing. I lace my fingers through his, see smudges of purple blood on his knuckles. His or Corbin's, I don't know, but my chest tightens at the sight.

I tear my gaze from that blood and look up at Will's face instead, into those eyes of flickering light and unfathomable depths. And I tell myself this is right. Will. Me. *Us*—on this journey together.

In moments, we're moving, the four most unlikely companions heading down the mountain, cutting through thinning mists . . . Nidia's shield of protection evaporating as we descend.

Away from the pride.

27

The last time I fled the pride there was only despair. Desolation in the belief that I would never be whole again. That without the pride, I would be nothing. It wasn't me fleeing, but Mom making me go.

This time is different. Now *I'm* fleeing. Me. Willingly. As fast as I can. Without the pride, I'm free. Whole as I haven't been in weeks. Hope overflows in my heart.

Will holds my hand between us. Cassian and Tamra are silent in the backseat. Tension swirls around the four of us as thick as the mists we leave behind.

I sense Cassian behind me. Angry-hard determination ripples off him. It mingles with my own lighter emotions. I focus on my feelings and fight to shove Cassian's away.

I look down at Will's hand wrapped around my own. So strong. I remember Corbin's bewilderment at his strength, and I let that settle in, sink deep. I'd seen evidence of it before. When he fought with Cassian on Big

Rock he held his own. I chalked it up to his training but now I'm not so sure. Not after today. Not after what I saw him do with the ground.

Is there some way Will gained multiple draki talents through the transfusion? The strength of an onyx draki *and* the power to manipulate ground and earth like an earth draki? Too incredible, maybe . . . but I know what I saw. He leveraged the earth. Just like an earth draki can do. I didn't imagine it.

Tamra witnessed it, too. It all goes back to the blood. It has to. What other explanation can there be? He's immune to shading, he's extraordinarily strong, he can manipulate the earth . . . That's more than any one single draki can do.

And I begin to wonder . . . what else hides in him? In his blood?

I want to talk to him about this, but only when we're alone. Knowing how Cassian feels, I don't want to bring up my suspicions that Will gained something more than a second lease on life through his transfusions.

I mull this over in the prolonged silence.

Conversation breaks out once, when Cassian asks, 'How long will it take to get there?'

'Depends if we drive straight through,' Will answers.

'We'll drive straight through,' Cassian returns flatly.

I glance at Will, notice a muscle feathering the flesh of his taut cheek. I give his fingers a slight squeeze, urging patience. This adventure is going to be hard enough. We should all try to get along.

Tamra snorts and mutters, 'Always in command.'

I glance back at her. She sits with her arms crossed, pressed against the door to get as far from Cassian as possible in the confines of the vehicle. I turn back around and blow out a slow breath.

It's going to be a long journey.

We drive for several hours, stopping only once for gas and food. I doze fitfully in the front seat, smoky, terror-soaked images flashing through my half-conscious mind.

I'm in the van again. With Miram. It's hot and airless and my pores scream for relief in the tight space. Moans choke Miram and I make my way to her on my hands and knees. Only when I touch her shoulder and roll her over, it's not Miram at all.

It's Dad.

His eyes are glassy, staring into nothing. No matter how I call him and shake him, he won't wake. He just lies there like a slab of cold stone.

I wrench myself fully awake, gasping.

Will's there, his hand closing over mine. 'You OK?'

I blink off the vestiges of sleep and nod, unable to hide how much the dream disturbed me. Glancing around, I notice we've stopped. He's standing outside the car and leaning over me.

'W-where are we? What are we doing?'

'Stopping for the night,' Will says. I peer through the darkness and notice Cassian's figure etched against the night. 'C'mon.'

I climb out of the car. Will takes my hand. The door slams as Tamra steps out, pulling her jacket close. 'It's cold.'

'I've got blankets, and we can start a fire.'

I shiver in the chilly night. It's colder here. I can already detect a drop in the temperature from when we last stopped several hundred miles south. In the distance, great jagged mountains, purple against the black night, break the sky.

Tamra blows into her hands. 'Can't we stay somewhere with a roof and four walls?'

'Until we're farther from the pride, we should stay low. Keep away from public places.'

I turn at Cassian's deep voice. His stare is liquid dark in the night. Unreadable as usual except *I* can read him. I can feel his anger. His sense of helplessness.

'He's right.' Will nods and it strikes me as odd that they're in accord over anything. 'Let's set up camp.'

'I'll gather firewood.' Cassian disappears into the trees, and I know he wants this. Time to himself. Away from the sight of me and Will.

Tamra and I help Will spread blankets on the ground and set up a ring of rocks for the fire. Will leaves and comes back with a bag of snacks we got from a gas station earlier. Tamra takes a bag of potato chips and drops down on a blanket.

Cassian returns and I pick a blanket to sit on, watching as he and Will work on getting a fire started. Again, this is strange, seeing them work side by side without trying to kill each other. And yet it gives me hope. Hope that we're going to band together and everything will be OK.

They're not having an easy time getting the fire to flourish—at least not quickly. I inch close and lean over the nest of sputtering flames and release enough steam so that the fire bursts to life. Will and Cassian jerk back.

Tamra laughs and edges closer, holding out her hands. 'Nice. Thought it was going to take them half the night.'

'Show-off,' Will murmurs, draping an arm around me. We settle back down onto the blanket and the chill melts away in his arms.

Cassian rustles through the bag of snacks. I watch him from the corner of my eye, sensing his discomfort. He selects a bottle of juice and fades into the trees. Part of me feels guilty, that I should go after him and try to ease his discomfort. We're bonded now. Fake or not, it can't be easy for him to watch me with Will.

But I've been gone too long from Will. I don't want to move, don't want to leave the comforting circle of his arms. Not yet. Not ever.

'Let's eat.' He stretches an arm and pulls the bag over to us. 'What's it going to be? Twinkies? Or Cheetos?'

I can't remember the last time I ate junk food. Not since Chaparral. I snatch the pack of Twinkies from his hand.

'I knew you'd pick that.'

'Why?'

His lips move over mine. 'Sweets for the sweet.'

Will takes care that I'm covered and pulls me close against his side. We share food and watch the gray clouds drift against the dark night. I drink strawberry soda until my nose tickles.

'I guess this is the date we never got a chance to have,' he murmurs, his breath warm on my cheek.

I smile, remembering that our first official date was interrupted by Xander and his cousins. 'Well, it's not that little Greek restaurant you promised me, but as far as dates go I'm having a pretty good time.'

'Strawberry soda, Twinkies, and Cheetos. You deserve better.'

Tamra groans and sits up, gathering her blanket and food. 'I'm going to sleep in the car. I can't survive a night of you two sweet talking.' She sends me a wink as she moves toward the car and I know that she's not really annoyed—that she's just giving us a chance to be alone.

We're quiet for several moments, wrapped in each other's arms, staring up at the night. 'We'll have that, Jacinda. Someday.'

I turn my face, almost bump my nose with his. 'What?'

'Normal dates.'

I smile. 'I'm not holding my breath for normal, Will. I just want us to be together. Safe. Happy.'

He runs his hand through my hair. 'We will be.'

We will be. After we reach the enkros stronghold and break out Miram. After we find Mom. I relax my thoughts, let them drift like the fast-moving clouds above. Will's fingers play gently in my hair. His touch lulls me.

'We're going to be fine. I'll get us in and out of there. I know how the enkros work.'

I know I should ask him to tell me more about them, to explain more about the enemy we face. I know I should tell him about Cassian and me bonding, but my eyes grow heavy even as I try to keep them open. My last sight is of Will, eyes wide-open, staring up at the night.

I wake with a shiver—mine or Will's, I can't tell for certain. We're tangled in each other's arms; where one of us ends and the other begins is hard to determine. I wiggle free from the comfort of his body and rouse the fire back to life with one gust of breath. Crouching there, I sweep my eyes over our little campsite and notice that it's still just Will and me.

Rising, I move to the car and spot my sister asleep in the back, the blanket pulled to her chin. No Cassian. The night is gray-blue in color. Dawn isn't too far off. Did he stay away all night?

Frowning, I head in the direction he took. The dense forest immediately swallows me. I'm not scared, though. Not of nature or my solitude within it. My strides eat up the forest floor, moist earth cushioned with pine needles. Twigs crunch beneath my shoes and the cracking sound gains a rhythm.

I move without thought, but my course is set, routed somewhere deep in my subconscious as I weave a purpose-filled path through the thick press of trees. I'm led by my sense of Cassian. He's somewhere close. I feel this. Feel him. In the distance, thunder rumbles softly.

The snap is subtle. There are so many sounds around me that I don't pay it much attention. Noises are part of the woods.

And then it comes again.

Without actually stopping, I listen, angling my face. Several twigs and leaves break beneath the pressure of something heavy. It's no small animal. No squirrel running through the undergrowth. Not Cassian.

The flesh at my nape quivers. I stop, hold my breath, and scan the ghostly shapes of the trees on every side of me. Releasing the breath I hold in my lungs, I ease down, squatting low, making myself as small as possible.

My fingers graze the ground, preparing to push off, bolt if needed. My bones begin the familiar pull, skin straining, itching to fade out and make way for my tougher draki skin.

The sound grows louder, stomping through the foliage.

Holding myself still, shrinking small, I become part of the landscape as I wait.

At last, I see the source of the noise.

A magnificent black bear lumbers between two trees, his shiny nose snuffling low to the ground as he makes his way. The creature lifts his shiny dark head, ears perked, nostrils working as he sniffs me out, scenting the air. He detects me.

With a huff the massive bear takes several aggressive steps in my direction. I rise to my feet, hold his stare, let him sense the animal in me . . . that I'm a creature like him, ready to fight back. He dips his head, ready to charge. Our stares lock for a breathless moment. Adrenaline pumps through me fast and hard.

Suddenly there's another sound. Cassian crashes through the trees, shouting my name as he arrives at my side. He grabs my hand. A rumbling growl erupts from Cassian's chest. A quick glance at his face reveals that he's half manifested. The vertical slits of his dragon eyes shudder with menace. His raw power feeds into me, makes me feel stronger. Together, we face the bear, a united front.

A moment passes as the bear continues to size us up. With a grunt, his dark, intelligent eyes slide away. He turns and continues on his way, foraging for more interesting material. I breathe easier watching him depart, admiring the ripple of his muscles beneath his thick coat of fur, relieved that neither one of us had to destroy the beautiful animal.

A smile curves my mouth as I turn to face Cassian. And that's when I see Will. He stands just beyond us, watching us with a look I've never seen. Doubt. Hurt. It's all there, passing over the carved lines of his face.

I tug my hand free from Cassian and slide it against my thigh, as if I could rub out the sensation of his touch.

'Will—' I stop myself just short of asking him how long he's been standing there, watching us. That would sound guilty, and I've done nothing wrong. *Nothing except hide the truth.*

Will points at Cassian. 'How did you know she was in trouble? You were barely in the campsite for five seconds before you took off, shouting that Jacinda was in trouble . . . you *knew*. How?'

I stare back and forth between Cassian and Will. Cassian looks at me, conveying that this is for me to explain.

'Jacinda,' Will says my name with heavy emphasis, waiting for an answer. For the truth, as much as I don't want it to be.

Closing my eyes, I fill my lungs with air. I knew I would have to tell him what happened at some point. 'Something happened when I went back home.'

Wariness glimmers in Will's eyes and I think he probably has a good idea of what I'm going to say. Or at least that he's not going to like it. 'What?'

'They decided to clip my wings.'

A muscle flickers in his jaw. 'Did they hurt you?'

I shake my head. 'No, but Mom protested and they banished her.'

'And? What else?' he prompts, knowing there's more, that I've left out the hard part. 'How come they didn't go through with it and clip your wings?'

I rush out with the rest, thinking the faster I say it, the better, the less painful. 'They changed their minds when Cassian offered an alternative.'

'An alternative?' Will no longer looks at me. He just locks gazes with Cassian. His profile hardens, as though he's bracing himself.

I swallow against the lump in my throat. 'Yes. As an alternative . . . he suggested that we bond.'

'Bond?' His gaze whips back to me. 'As in marriage?'

'For the draki, yes, it's much the same thing.' Only the connection can be *more*, can run deeper than that, can link a couple emotionally . . .

None of this I say. Not yet. *Let him digest one thing at a time.*

He swings around and walks a hard line, stopping near a tree. I stare helplessly at the rigid line of his back, jump as he suddenly moves, slamming his fist into the rough bark.

I move forward, grip his arm with desperate fingers. 'It was either a fake bonding or the wing clipping.' I take his hand, examine the torn and bleeding knuckles with a hiss. 'Please understand, Will.'

He blows a deep breath and nods slowly, turning around. 'I understand. I do.' Only he doesn't stare at me. He looks beyond my shoulder at Cassian. 'And I don't blame you, Jacinda. A fake bonding,' he echoes with a sharp nod of his head. 'It's not real.'

My chest eases, feels less tight. Will understands. We're going to be OK. We're going to be fine. I believe this. Until Cassian's deep voice intrudes and the smile slips from my lips.

'Since you've started, why not tell him everything, Jacinda?'

I glare at Cassian.

'What are you leaving out?' Will asks, his fingers loosening around mine, and I hate that, hate that he's pulling away from me.

I snatch his hand back and tighten my hold. 'Nothing. You know everything.' Everything that isn't superstitious nonsense. Not every draki couple forms a connection. It's not an absolute. Why should I bring it up? Just because I imagine that I have a better read on Cassian's emotions lately? Just because he sensed I might be in danger?

'He wanted to know how I knew you were in trouble. Tell him why, Jacinda.'

Tension radiates from Will. He stands like a wire pulled tight, about to spring apart.

'Some say—' I clear my throat. 'Some believe that once a draki couple bond a . . . connection is formed.'

'Connection?' Will cocks his head and something is inherently dangerous in the gesture, like he might spring into attack.

'An emotional connection,' I elaborate.

At first Will doesn't speak, looks straight ahead at Cassian before he repeats, '*Some* believe? What do *you* believe? What's true, Jacinda?'

'Well, it's different for everyone. Not—'

'And how is it for the two of you?'

I flinch at the lash of his voice. 'It's—' I *want* to lie. I don't want to hurt him, but most of all I don't want him to think that he and I are anything *less* than before I bonded to Cassian. Because it *can't* be true.

And yet I can't lie. Not to Will.

With a swallow, I admit, 'Since the bonding . . . there is something there. I've been more attuned to Cassian.'

Will nods slowly and edges away from me.

'What are you doing?' I demand with a touch of panic as he begins walking away from me.

Oh, hell, no. I haven't gone through everything just so he can quit on us now. I turn on Cassian. 'Are you happy?'

Cassian shakes his head, and what infuriates me even more is the pity I read in his eyes. 'He had to be told. I'm sorry, Jac—'

'Don't,' I bite out. 'Don't feel sorry for me. I don't need your pity. Will and I are going to be fine.'

With that declaration, I take off after Will. He's walking fast, cutting a swift path through the trees.

'Hey! You know there's a bear out here somewhere,' I shout in warning.

He doesn't respond.

'Will! Where are you going?'

I race to keep up with him. Grabbing his arm, I'm prepared to force him around when he whirls to face me.

'What am I supposed to do, Jacinda?' he explodes. 'Wear a smile on my face knowing you've bonded with Cassian and, oh, by the way, that pretty much means you're automatically in love with him?'

'That's not what I said!' I flap my arms. 'That's *not* true!'

'Why don't you explain it to me then?' He crosses his arms over his broad chest. 'What else does emotionally connected mean?'

'Well, I would explain it if you weren't being such a jerk!' I jab him in the chest.

He stares down at me for a long moment. A smile plays on his mouth. 'OK. Explain.'

'Since we've bonded I've just had a better read on him . . . I can sometimes sense, feel what he's feeling. That's it. That's *all*.'

'You go around feeling what he's feeling all the time?'

'Well, only the really intense emotions. Not every little thing.'

245

He still looks uncertain, so I step closer and soften my voice, trace my fingers along his tense forearm. 'This doesn't change how I feel about you.'

He steps back and drops his arms, severing our contact.

I won't let him retreat from me. We've come too far. I'll fight for us even if it's him I have to fight. 'It doesn't affect how I feel for you. Are you going to let it affect how *you* feel?'

He looks down at me, his gaze a dark glitter in the night. I can't read him. I step close, brush his hand with mine, just the slightest graze of our fingers . . . testing.

His pinky finger loops with mine and the breath I'd been holding escapes in a hush, the ache in my heart easing a bit.

'I'm here,' I remind. 'With you. I left Cassian with the pride. He wasn't part of my escape plan, remember?'

Will sighs and drags a hand through his hair. 'Yeah. I know. God, Jacinda, I'm just ready for us to be together . . . with nothing getting in the way.'

I step into his arms. 'We are. From now on. We're not going to be apart ever again. We're going to break Miram out and then it'll be the two of us.'

'The two of us. That'd be nice.'

I exhale in relief, the insane urge to cry coming over me. Until now I didn't realize just how worried I was that he'd turn his back on me for good when I told him the truth. It confirms everything I ever thought about him, validates that this is right. Him. *Us.*

We stand together, clinging to each other for several minutes. Two honks finally draw us apart.

'Tamra,' I guess.

'All right. Let's go.' Will takes my hand and leads me to the waiting car.

'Did you two make up?' Tamra asks when we're back inside. Either she heard the shouting or Cassian caught her up to speed.

'We're fine,' I say, sending Tamra a warning look to drop the subject.

'We're *good*,' Will adds, looking meaningfully at Cassian. Cassian stares back unperturbed.

'Good.' Tamra nods. 'Let's get going. The sooner we rescue the little witch, the sooner we're free.'

I don't bother asking free from what. Or from whom. For Tamra it's become all the same. The pride. Cassian.

Soon we're moving back down the highway, plunging headlong into the sunrise.

28

Several hours later, after we've ditched Will's car for a van that's seen better days, I shoot a glance over my shoulder at Cassian and Tamra asleep in the back, lying on blankets they spread out on the rusted and dented floor.

'How much longer?' I whisper.

'Maybe tomorrow night. If we drive through and don't stop.'

'Good.'

The floorboard rumbles beneath the soles of my shoes and I curl my knees to my chest. Shifting on the torn vinyl seat, I try not to miss the comfortable seat of Will's Land Rover. It's only temporary. We parked his car at a truck stop, ready for us to reclaim after we rescue Miram.

Sighing, I lean my head back on the headrest. The sooner we do this, the sooner Miram and Cassian go home. The sooner Will, Tamra, and I can find Mom and start over someplace else. I stare through the window, almost relieved to see the clear night all around us. No perpetual mist.

Will reaches for my hand. His thumb traces the inside of my wrist. Sparks ignite up my arm from the simple touch. We share a heated look, and I know he feels it, too. Slipping a glance over my shoulder at the sleeping pair in the back, I acknowledge it might be a while before we have some privacy, and this bothers me. We're heading into danger. We might not make it out.

As though he senses my doubts, he says, 'I've done the drop before with my father. It's easy enough getting in.'

'It's not getting in I'm worried about.'

'We'll get out. They'll never suspect a hunter ever wanting to break a draki out. We drop, we get paid, we leave.' He nods once, and I'm not sure whether he believes what he's saying or not. 'We'll escape. And then we'll be together. Without Cassian.'

The headlights of an oncoming car light up Will's face. If his words weren't enough, his intense expression drives home for me that he might not blame me for the bonding, but he's not at peace with it either. He'll never be at peace until Cassian's back with the pride and I'm . . . *not*.

'I told you it's not real.'

'I know. You were forced into it. It means nothing.' He brings my hand to his lips for a tender kiss. 'Why don't you get some sleep?'

'Sure you're not too tired to drive?'

'Cassian offered to take the wheel for a while. I'll wake him in an hour.'

Closing my eyes, I'm convinced I can never sleep.

That's my last thought.

* * *

A firm hand on my shoulder shakes me into consciousness. I jerk, looking around, every muscle tense, ready to defend, run, *fly.*

'We're here,' Will says.

When did I become so guarded, so braced for attack? I don't try to figure it out. Just tell myself this is good for the events to come.

I look left and right. We sit parked on a narrow dirt road, trees all around. Tamra leans forward between us and echoes my thoughts. 'There's nothing here.'

Will cocks his head. 'You didn't think I'd drive to the front gates and honk, did you?'

Tamra snorts. 'Well, show us then, fearless leader.'

I look almost in bewilderment at my sister. She acts like this is nothing. As if we're just out for the day, cruising the countryside or something.

Will steps from the van. Cassian's already outside, holding his face up to the breeze like he's scenting the air. I guess he probably is.

Will opens the back doors of the van and throws aside the blanket covering an array of weaponry. I'd already seen the arsenal when we switched vehicles, but the sight still makes me inhale sharply.

Cassian immediately starts handling weapons, deciding which one to take, and I watch, amazed as he and Will revert to guy talk over the variety of guns, knives and bows, weighing the pros and cons like old comrades.

Tamra and I roll our eyes at each other.

After a few moments, I clear my throat. 'Are we going in there guns blazing or something?'

'Yeah,' Tamra agrees. 'I thought this was just supposed to be a surveillance run first. So we can get a feel for the place.'

'It is. This is just a precaution.' Will straps an ankle holster beneath his jean leg, slipping a gun inside. I shiver a little at his smooth movements, reminded that he's done this before. Cassian follows suit, and I stop myself from asking whether he even knows how to shoot a gun. They're not part of our life in the pride. But something stops me. For once, the guys are in accord. I don't want to ruin that.

Will selects four binoculars and hands one to each of us. He gives me a wink. 'We'll look over the layout for now, and then come up with our strategy.'

Slamming the doors shut, he leads us off the road. Tall grass snags at my jeans as we move through the shadows of trees, almost like grasping hands trying to stop us.

The air is colder here than even I'm used to, and I snuggle into my fleece jacket. For the first time in my life I might actually need a parka.

The trees begin to thin. Will holds up a hand. We stop. 'From here we crawl,' he says, nodding ahead to where there's nothing but a sloping field. 'They have lookouts. They're always watching. Even when you can't see them. We don't need to be spotted.'

My skin is tight and prickly as we crawl on our hands and knees, moving downhill. We finally stop, perched on a rise. Below, a small town sits nestled in a valley.

'What is this place?' Tamra asks, peering out with her binoculars.

'Crescent Valley,' Will answers. 'Population: nine hundred and seventy-eight.'

'It looks dead,' Cassian observes.

'Pretty much,' Will agrees, gesturing to the picturesque valley below. 'The grocery store. Crescent Valley

School—all grade levels in one building. The community hall. Joel's Bar and Grill. Antonio's over there serves a decent pizza. I've waited there when my dad and uncle made drops. No more than two can drop off. And there, see that big building? That's the number one employer in town—CVMS. Crescent Valley Medical Suppliers.'

I survey the innocuous sprawling factory of dingy white rock. Less innocuous is the high fence with its winding ropes of barbed wire along the top. A uniformed guard stands at a gatehouse. It's the only way in or out that I can detect. The vast parking lot is half full, dotted with cars.

'They sell mostly medical supplies. Stuff used in your standard doctor's office. Syringes. Some surgical equipment.'

'*This* is the enkros stronghold?' Cassian asks. 'It's a front?'

'Yes,' Will answers, his lips pressing into a grim line. He gestures to the entire valley with his hand. 'All of it is. The whole town. Everyone is connected or related to someone who works there.'

My skin hums itchy-hot, heart hammering in my chest as I look down at the valley, at the place I had feared for so many years while knowing so little about it, without having any notion what it could be.

This is ten times worse than the prisonlike fortress I imagined. It's evil wrapped up in innocent packaging.

It sits there, tidy bows and all, within a seemingly normal community. Underneath it all, it's a place of torment and death.

My father's image swims before my eyes. Is this where they took him? And Miram? Are they both behind those walls?

Resolve rolls through me in a bitter wash. Mine. Cassian's. It doesn't matter really. In this, we feel the same. Suddenly it's about more than rescuing Miram.

I sense Will's gaze on my face and turn to him. He knows. He's with me. We're together in this. In everything.

'Let's bring it down,' I mutter. 'All of it.'

He smiles and warmth spreads through me at how fortunate I am, how far I have come. I have Will. I have my sister. I even have Cassian. I'm not going into this alone, a victim like Miram. A captive like Dad. We will infiltrate the stronghold. We will rescue Miram. We will stand together. Right now, I'm convinced anything is possible.

Desperate to know what happens next?

Find out in the dramatic conclusion to the Firelight sequence

Hidden

ALL WILL BE REVEALED...

September 2013

978-0-19-275656-5

About the Author

SOPHIE JORDAN grew up on a pecan farm in the Texas hill country, where she wove fantasies of dragons, warriors, and princesses. A former high school English teacher, she's also the *New York Times* bestselling author of historical romances. She now lives in Houston with her family. When she's not writing, she spends her time overloading on caffeine (lattes and Diet cherry Coke preferred) and talking plotlines with anyone who will listen (including her kids). Sophie also writes paranormal romances under the name Sharie Kohler.

You can visit her online at *www.sophiejordan.net*.